SEA-SIDE CITY
LIFE IN THE RUINS

S.A. BALLANTYNE

ISBN: 9798466159738

Alone with my woes,
All my friends turn to foes
While others sleep tight
I lose the will to fight.

Without the comfort of distraction
there is no satisfaction

The masks I wear,
cause inner conflict to flair
but the crosses I bear,
are lighter when others are there

- S.A. Ballantyne

DEDICATION

To My Girlfriend/ Better Half
Charlette

Thank you for being a beacon of light and positivity
through the dark and uncertain times of past present and
future.

PHOTO CREDITS

All images used in this project have either been taken by myself
or sourced through Canva Pro, Pixabay or Pexels.

Front Cover
Background: passigatti via Canva Pro
Hooded figure: Kuzmik_A via Canva Pro
Cover Designed by S.A. BALLANTYNE

Pg iii – thomaszsebok via Canva Pro
(recoloured& cropped by S.A. BALLANTYNE)

Pg 15 – Tama66 via Pixabay
(Recoloured and Cropped by S.A. BALLANTYNE)

Pg 25 – S.A. BALLANTYNE

Pg 33 –Plant Graphic: tony241969 via Canva Pro
Background: aleksandarstudio via Canva Pro
(Both images recoloured/arranged by S.A. BALLANTYNE)

Pg 48 – bortn76 via Canva Pro

Pg 61 – khunkorn via Canva Pro
(Cropped/ Recoloured by S.A. BALLANTYNE)

Pg 79 – Michael Gane via Canva Pro

Pg 94 – Jessica Zaccaria via Canva Pro
(Recoloured/Distorted by S.A. BALLANTYNE)

Pg 106 – Harun Tan via Pexels

Special Thanks to
MartynaMadege& Benfor advice and support on creating the
trailers.

CONTENTS

Acknowledgments   i

Chapter 1: Home   Pg 1

Chapter 2: A Pilgrimage through Purgatory   Pg 16

Chapter 3: Consumed   Pg 26

Chapter 4: Assess and Repair   Pg 34

Chapter 5: Touching Base   Pg 49

Chapter 6: Roots   Pg 62

Chapter 7: The Hope Centre   Pg 80

Chapter 8: Return to the "Sea-Side City"   Pg 95

Aftermath   Pg 107

More from the Sea-Side City   Pg 112

Timeline   Pg 113

About NDP   Pg 114

Map of Rockshore   Pg 116

Next Story Preview   Pg 117

ACKNOWLEDGMENTS

Cover Photos: sourced from Canva pro
Cover Designed by: S.A. BALLANTYNE

Firstly I'd like to thank my mother (Lorraine) and my girlfriend (Charlette). Both of you have been incredibly supportive and loving: especially throughout this (self-inflicted) hectic time in my life.

Special thanks to David S Carlin
& my many other amazing friends
The Costers (Ty, Boris, Chrissy, Tilly and Rosie)
Danny, Ollie, Ant, Jack, Martin, Tamara Craig, Clarissa, Tom, Grace, Josie, Gemma, Hetti, Josh, Lozz, Lloyd, James.

Additionally I'd like to thank a number of people who have motivated, inspired and assisted me at the right points in life:
Pete Bolton, Steve Tansey, Graham Brooks, Lindsey Smith, Mike Lever, Peter Palmer, Andy Simmonz, Nathan Mackenzie, Jon Patterson, Pat Davis, Jamie Howard, Mary Lenton, Keith Coleman,& David Taylor-Jones.

I would also like to thank you for taking the time to read

SEA-SIDE CITY
LIFE IN THE RUINS

-S.A. BALLANTYNE

CHAPTER 1:
HOME?

In amongst the civilised confines of the Coastal Collage shopping centre, Max nervously paced around trying to camouflage his criminal intentions from those around him. However, the toll his lifestyle had taken on his appearance, made his intentions increasingly more obvious to the general public. The once healthy young man was now reduced to a soulless husk of his former self; with malnourished acne filled skin, rotting teeth and glazed bloodshot eyes.

The Coastal Collage was a stylish indoor shopping centre, known for its innovative architecture and relaxing indoor neon lighting. Its front entrance had a multi-coloured glass arch which illuminated the floor below it in technicolour and attracted passers-by to frequent the wide variety of shops inside.

Max had intended to wait for the right moment to seize

something of value and flee the premises undetected. Unfortunately, his addiction took control, rendering him powerless to its unforgiving hold on his body and his mind. Clutching and scratching at his arms, his eyes darted around the colourful shopping centre, desperately looking for a means of facilitating his next fix.

Suddenly, he heard a female voice behind him;

"Yeah hun, I'll be round at 7 don't worry."

Oblivious to the primitive threat in front of her, she continued to chat to her friend on her phone. Max turned to her immediately and grabbed her handbag from her shoulder.

The primal force in which he used to snatch the bag knocked the woman off her feet. Shocked and horrified by what was happening to her, the woman cried for help. Upon hearing her scream, the amateur mugger turned back to face his fallen victim, unconcerned for her wellbeing or the depths to which he'd sunk, he opportunistically grabbed the phone from the floor and continued to flee. A shop security guard spotted the commotion and gave chase.

Filled with adrenaline, Max continued to sprint as fast as he could. It wasn't long before he had managed to lose the security guard and escape the building. The security guard radioed over to other personnel in the area, then turned his attentions to the victim of the mugging.

After successfully escaping the shopping centre, the desperately deranged young man continued to sprint through the city centre. Once he reached the Town Square, he felt assured he had escaped the threat of the Coastal Collage security team. He laughed manically with tears in his eyes, rubbing and clasping at his face with the palms of his hands, in a frantic celebration of his successful loot. Realising he still had a considerable journey to make, the fiend scanned the area with his red bloodshot eyes. Donning his hood and pulling the drawstrings he jogged through the back alleys. He made a conscious effort to avoid Penelope Park which was occupied by the Sea-Side Saxons, who kept a vigilant watch for criminal activity.

Max continued on through the back alleys, continuously turning back to check if he was being followed. At this point in time he had managed to evade the threat of authority figures in the City Centre area. However, due to the paranoia his addiction subjected him to, he was unable to shake the feeling of being watched and followed. Continuing to stagger through the back alleys, it wasn't long before he reached the depraved area of 'Jacksville'. Despite the area being an epicentre of crime and anti-social behaviour, it was a mere passing place on Max's journey. Clutching his freshly stolen handbag and phone, the journey continued. At this point, nausea started to take its effect on his body. Even though it was a mild day in the earlier part of April, Max's body temperature fluctuated from one moment to the next.

As the hellish effects of addiction and withdrawal circulated his body internally, the threat of external dangers also started to emerge. A pair of thuggish looking men approached. Although they were keeping to themselves, as Max drew nearer, they became increasingly alerted to the state he was in.

"Look at this dirty smackhead!" one of them snarled. Upon further observation, the second man commented;

"He's got a handbag! Scatty rat's thieved it!"

Grimacing at the decadent sight before their eyes, the men approached him. Although they hadn't vocalised their intentions, they planned to pummel him and take the bag and any other valuables he had for their own gain. Despite his condition, Max was aware of the men's presence. Once their paths met, he tried to scurry past them. The man closest to him intercepted him and shoved him into the wall.

"Nice bag love, where'd you get it?"

the attacker sneered as his malnourished frame hit the

wall.

"Agh! It's my mum's I swear; please don't take it, she loves it mate!"

Max grovelled, desperate to maintain his means of getting his fix. He staggered back against the wall trying to create distance.

"GIVE IT HERE YOU THEIVING RAT!" The second man commanded.

Max's heart rate increased and his breath quickened, scrambling to prevent them from taking it. He retrieved a shiv from the pocket of his torn tracksuit pocket. He held the blade outwards with his left hand, clasping the bag tightly to his chest with his right arm. The two men were un-intimidated and readying themselves to attack. Suddenly, Max fell to the floor doubled over. He started to wretch, subsequently vomiting all over the bag. Disgusted and outraged the men backed away.

"Aw, dirty scumbag." One of them exclaimed. The other snarled

"Next time I see this melt I'm going to do him in proper!"

Unwilling to further pursue a conflict with the vomit covered junkie, the pair of thugs took their leave. Once Max's body enabled him to muster enough energy, he staggered back to his feet

Clutching the bag to his chest, he put his shiv back into his tattered, torn and dirty tracksuit. Luckily, there didn't seem to be anybody else around the vicinity. He proceeded to negotiate his way through Jacksville, shiftily sneaking through the back alleys behind the estates. Although it only took around ten minutes, it felt like an eternity before he reached the reassuring sight of "The Rough Tide" Public House. It was a landmark that very few people in Rockshore would have been pleased to see. However, for Max it signified that he had almost reached the conclusion of his journey, South Town Harbour.

The condemned dock site of South Town Harbour was a

safe haven for drug fiends and an epicentre of criminal activity in the Sea-Side City. Sadly the morally depraved wasteland was also the closest thing Max now had to a home. Shivering and exhausted, the 20 yards between the Rough Tide Pub and the entrance to the harbour felt like an eternity away. Eventually, scurrying through a hole in the fence, similarly to a wharf-rat, he made it into the harbour. Max would soon join the other metaphoric vermin in the condemned area.

Even in the light of day, the atmosphere of South Town Harbour seemed insidious and unsettling. Upon entering the concrete wasteland the stench of old urine pungently polluted the air. At first glance, it simply looked like the derelict site it was advertised to be.

Broken appliances were piled up to the left and a fire damaged old brick building to the right. If an unsuspecting member of the public poked their head through the fence, they would most probably assume that it was uninhabited. As Max ventured past the junk site and deeper down the cobbled walkway, it would be clear to all who entered that they were somewhere they didn't want to be. The ground and walls were sporadically splattered with dried blood, warning of the feral violence that would occur in the territory. Max had been numbed to the sights and smells of South-Town Harbour for some time. He was there out of necessity, so deep in his addiction that he had nowhere else to go.

Turning to his right he made his way into a seemingly abandoned old building. The door creaked open as he staggered in, shaking and still clutching at his vomit stained bag. Although the building appeared bare and dusty, there were a number of prone bodies passed out on the floor. The unnerving combination of murmurs, groans and snoring could be heard around the room. Max cautiously crept through the room trying not to alert them to his presence, fearful of potential threats to his loot.

Finally reaching a staircase, he scurried up the wooden

steps. Suddenly, in his haste, Max's foot broke through the last step.

He cried out in agony. He had sprained his ankle. Falling to the floor, he pulled his foot out of the hole. Upon pulling it out the shards of wood ripped his tracksuit and torn into his skin.

"What the hell's that bloody noise?!"An irritable voice enquired.

It was Candy-Shilling, the drug baron who managed and profited from the illegal activity in South Town Harbour. The tattered middle aged man was sat in a filthy office chair at his broken desk. Arising from his chair and leaning over the desk, Candy-Shilling scrutinised Max. His sight was limited due to only having one functioning eye; the other was behind an eye patch.

He grimaced in anger, showing his rotten teeth, snarling;

"Get up of your arse and shut up, before you wind the rest of them up!"

Following the disgusting gangster's instructions, the helpless slave dragged himself away from the stairs and towards the desk. As he got closer, Candy-Shilling started to recognise him. He started to cackle;

"Ah it's my dear Maxine, with a new handbag. It looks like this little bird's hurt her leg too."

Indifferent to his injury or Candy-Shilling's taunting, Max limped over to the desk presenting the bag.

The arrangement was that he would supply his addicts with their drug of choice in exchange for money or valuables. Candy-Shilling inspected the bag and its contents. It wasn't long before he reached a conclusion;

"This is tat mate, worthless! It stinks of puke and there's no money in it."

Upon hearing that his ill-gotten gains were inadequate, Max immediately retrieved the stolen phone from his pocket. Candy-Shilling snatched it from him; the wily gangster quickly established that the phone's screen was broken.

"Oh dearie, dearie me, well unless you can pull something more valuable or some cash out 'your arse, there'll be no candy for you today. It looks like you've wasted your time dearie. More importantly though, you've wasted my time!"

Despairing at the state his life had got to, Max tearfully clutched at his head. He desperately pleaded;

"Please mate, I'll go out and do some deals. Just give me..." before he could finish, Candy-Shilling snarled;

"Oh piss off! Do you think I'm some sort of a mug? I'm not giving you nothing until you earn it."

Suffering the effects of his withdrawals, he unexpectedly started to laugh manically.

"I don't need it anyway, I'm just going to quit."

Having witnessed similarly erratic reactions before, the callous gangster cackled;

"Course' you are mate, bloody hell I ain't heard that one in a while. You're body's just going off its nut, cause' you ain't got what you need..."

As he lurched over his desk, taunting his consumed consumer, Candy-Shilling's attentions were turned to the broken stair. His jovial mood instantly soured as he saw the blood stains and shards of wood in Max's injured leg

"You arsehole! You absolute arsehole! You've put a bloody hole in my stairs.

Bugger the drugs; you're going to be working tonight to pay off a maintenance debt. Question is are you going to be making someone rich, or making someone twitch?" Max's face dropped with the realisation of his undesirable ultimatum.

He would either have to enter into the fighting ring, or prostitute himself that evening. Naturally, Candy-Shilling had no intention of paying to have the stairs repaired. Rather he would take any opportunity to extort extra money from whoever he could.

After creating a surge in drug users across the city he would use their habits against them to do his bidding and facilitate his financial plans.

Max limped back down the stairs, still riddled with the hellish effects of his dehumanizing habits. Candy-Shilling bellowed after him;

"You'd better be in either the tower or the motel when the punters get here in two hours. If not we'll do you in!"

The "punters" he was referring to was a selection of undesirables from around the area who would sneak into the harbour after hours. Some travelled over from Cockleshell Island via boat.

Due to the condemned harbour's lack of security, they would use the crumbling port decks to dock their boats. In the city's neglect, Candy-Shilling had essentially converted the harbour into a criminal entertainment complex. Max left the confines of the port house and hobbled around the harbour, much like a zombie, unable to rest but unable to live. Looking out beyond the crumbling docks to the sea, he continued to gingerly wander down the cobbled path which led deeper into the bowels of the harbour.

The cobbles in the path once clean and well maintained now covered in filth and vomit. Max found himself strolling towards what Candy-Shilling referred to as the "Shag Pile"; an avenue with a large warehouse factory with shutters and broken windows. The warehouse had several old broken beds and mattresses, which had been left around the harbour or fly tipped. Above the shutter door on the outside of the warehouse, the sign had been amended to read "Shag Pile - Whorehouse", through the use of graffiti.

The addicts would prostitute themselves to support their addictive habits. Naturally Candy-Shilling would get the money funnelled back to him, following the sale of various drugs.

Max started to shiver again, becoming agitated at the thought of how long it would take for his next fix.

He didn't want to have to sell himself to whoever wanted him. However, with his newly acquired ankle injury, he wouldn't last long in a fight.

"Oi, what you doing here? You finally out of money?" A voice interrupted Max's fragmented wanderings. Before Max could register who was speaking, a female emerged from the adjacent wall to the warehouse. It was a woman named "Sledge". She was in charge of overseeing the frequenters, ensuring that they paid an entrance toll (which was also split with Candy-Shilling).

Sledge put out her cigarette on the cobbled pathway and walked towards Max. Wearing a grey hoodie and a torn dress, her shoes clopped across the concrete as she neared.

"You gonna answer me rich boy?"

Sledge questioned irritably as she pushed him against the wall. Max mumbled, trying to explain his unenviable dilemma. Disinterested, Sledge interrupted once again;

"Yeah mate, whatever, you can work here tonight or you can go and get what's left of your teeth smashed in over in the fight tank. We don't have many lads working here, but you're still going to get the standard rate, it makes no difference to me."

With that, Sledge continued into the warehouse, leaving Max to further contemplate his options.

Unfortunately, the madam's comments about Max being a "rich boy" traced his mind back to happier and much less desperate times. Like so many others who had succumb to addictions of this nature, Max did not start out this way. He came from a middle class family who supported his education. He had been raised to be financially savvy and save as much money as he could. Due to this fact, it had taken him a longer time to inevitably lose everything to his addiction.

He stared blankly into a broken pine bookshelf left on the side of the cobbled street. It reminded him of the bookshelf in his childhood bedroom. His mind was taken back to his youth. He remembered sitting in his room listening to music after school. He vividly recalled sitting cross legged in his school uniform on his bedroom floor. Although he was encouraged by his parents to get changed

9

out of his uniform as quickly as possible, the privacy his room provided allowed him the freedom to ignore the nagging feeling telling him to get changed and peacefully sit listening to old songs on the radio. He remembered the aroma of fresh home cooking emerging from the kitchen. The more time he spent in the seemingly random memory, the more Max started to yearn for the security and unlimited potential of his earlier life.

As he started to remember his mother, father and sister, Max's attention was drawn back to his body's cravings. His memories of a carefree life became more of a distant fantasy. The harsh realities of his dependant lifestyle reeled him back into the unsavoury confines of South Town Harbour.

By this time, the evening was closing in. Soon it would be time for Max to decide between spending his night in the Shag Pile or the Fight Tank. After being haunted by his memories of happier times, Max felt a deep rage burning within him. His mind became tormented with one question, how could his life have turned out this way? The more he thought about it, the angrier he became. He found himself being drawn towards the Fight Tank.

The Fight Tank was held in a large fishery warehouse on the adjacent side of the cobbled street. Approaching the rusty steel open shutter doors, Max's temperature started to fluctuate from hot to cold. Upon entering, his sense of smell was hit by the aroma of sea-water and wet concrete. The warehouse echoed with the sounds of dripping water from its leaking metal roof. Directly in the centre of the intimidating steel structure, there was a 15x15 foot circular area cordoned by coils of large weathered, blood stained rope, iron fence posts and rusted chain.

In an attempt to ready himself for the brutality he would have to, both, endure and conjure to survive the night, Max approached the fight ring. With every step, his injured leg emitted pain. His attentions were drawn to a tooth in a small puddle outside of the fight ring. Just as he was about to slip into another trance, a hand reached down and picked up the tooth.

"You could lose a lot more than this if you hang around here too long. Punters will be here in about 10 minutes mate"The ringmaster warned, as he inspected the tooth.

Max irritably replied;

"I don't care, I'm gonna do what I've got to do."

Slowly drawing his attention from the tooth to Max, the ringmaster looked him up and down, he scoffed;

"Yeah, okay mate."

The ringmaster had become underwhelmed and numb to the delusional claims of drug addicts and desperados indebted to Candy-Shilling. Like so many others both inside and outside the harbour, the ringmaster's primary interest was making money. When he looked at someone like Max, all he could see was the odds of their success or failure in combat. Knowing the condition of the junkies within the harbour, he would spend most of the time estimating the odds of the combatants going down in one punch or being knocked out due to their coordination.

Max was not deterred by the ringmaster's dismissive attitude. He could hear the nearing sound of boat engines approaching the docks. He climbed the steps to the balcony to see the incoming fleet, leaning heavily on the rusty stair rail to alleviate the pressure on his ankle. Two small dinghies had docked up and four larger boats were making their way towards the docks. Several men got out of the boats, each of them wearing mismatched clothing and jewellery. A large tattooed man wearing a vest, a leather jacket and a gold chain around his neck ordered the others to tie up the boat.

Max's eyes wandered to the rest of the incoming convoy. Suddenly, another boat caught his eye, a stationary sailing vessel which had been docked to conceal the other boats from public view. The shape of the boat and its weathered white sails reminded Max of an indoor play centre his parents took him to during his childhood. "Jolly Roger's

Play Boat" was one of his favourite places in his earlier years.

*DONG

Max's thoughts were disrupted by his environment once again; someone had thrown a rock which hit the metallic wall a few feet above him. He looked down at the crowd which had gathered near the fight ring. Laughter and jeers echoed around the warehouse.

"Oi junkie! If you're fighting, get your arse down here. If you're not, piss off!"

The ringmaster called up to him.

Max had become numb; he hobbled down the staircase still favouring his injured ankle. The pain increased with each step, he began to feel adrenaline course through his body. Making his way through the increasing crowd, he could hear the punters heckling and taunting him. Each of them made snide remarks about his gaunt appearance, weight and unintimidating presence. The more they taunted, the angrier he felt. Finally, he made it through the hostile audience to the jagged and intimidating confines of the fight ring.

The ringmaster announced;

"Alright ladies and gents, coming in first is… Scrawny! Who's got money on Scrawny?"

Max looked to the ringmaster and his blackboard. Naturally the odds for him to win were unfavourable. However, despite the odds being named "Scrawny", he was still optimistic. From a strategic standpoint, this would prove that he could work off his debt to Candy-Shilling in less time. Within a few minutes his opponent was announced.

"Coming in second….Tweaker!

Place your bets on Tweaker."

Following his announcement, an older man shuffled in. The man's skin was discoloured and stained with dried dirt. His arms were covered in cuts, scrapes and needle marks.He rambled incoherently as he entered the area. Max felt incredibly uneasy. The sickening feeling of adrenaline coursing through his body, combined with his rage, fear and the pain from his injured ankle. Yet in addition to the intimidation he felt for the animalistic specimen which stood before him, he also felt a sense of moral discomfort. Even in his state of savage desperation, Max could see the pain and torment in his opponent. The man was clearly suffering from the withdrawals of his addiction, similarly to Max.

He paced frantically and foamed at the mouth while his body shook uncontrollably.

Several spectators crowded around the fight ring
aggressively and profanely encouraged him to attack Max.

Continuing to snarl, the deranged man lunged at him in a feral manner. The crowd became more excitable at the prospect of physical violence.

The adrenaline running through Max's body allowed him to react quickly, evading his attacker.

In missing his target, Max's opponent lost his balance, charging head first into the iron fence post. The impact caused the man's head to split open and fall on his face onto the rusting chains below.

Max's ankle gave out shortly after the motion. He fell back on his side next to his downed opponent. The crowd laughed and jeered at their botched fight. He noticed that the man wasn't moving as blood trickled down his head causing a pool of blood to cascade on the rope and chains below.

Thankful he had survived the encounter and eager to get out, Max pulled himself back to his feet exclaiming;

"He's out, cash me out!"

After a few long, painful seconds, the ringmaster announced that "Scrawny" was the winner. Just as Max was about to exit the ring, Candy-Shilling emerged from the crowd.

The old gangster angrily screeched,

"You're not done yet, you still owe me money!
Get back in there and work it off!"

The exhausted and desperate young man defensively protested,

"I'm done, I'll come back tomorrow!"

Suddenly, Max felt his body being pulled around by the crowd behind him. Turning back to face them, he recognised the large tattooed man that he had seen earlier, grimacing at him. The man sternly mumbled,

"Stop wasting our bloody time you scrawny flid!"

Following the man's verbal abuse, another member of the crowd blindsided Max with a right cross to the temple. The punch not only knocked Max to the ground, but it knocked him out. While his eyes were rolling to the back of his head and he started to lose consciousness, he heard the crowd roar in approval and Candy-Shilling bark something about working off the money he owed.

CHAPTER 2:
A PILGRIMAGE THROUGH PURGATORY

Several hours later, Max started to stir. His eyes opened periodically as he drifted in and out of consciousness. He slowly began to recognise traits of the room he was in. Laying face down on a bare mattress, the disorientated young man began to come to. His head was throbbing and his body was still feeling the effects of the harrowing toll the previous days had taken on it. He pushed himself up off the floor with his arms. Suddenly, he felt a sharp pain in his backside as he moved his legs. He exhaled in pain. Following his expression of discomfort, Sledge's hardened, husky voice quietly commented;

"Bloody hell, you're up early!"

She was leaning against the wall, smoking a cigarette and shivering with the briskness of the morning. Max's eyes became more sensitive to the daylight of the morning as he looked up at her. The more he began to come to his senses, the more discomfort he felt.

"What happened to me?" He moaned.

Although he couldn't see it, there was a rare glimmer of concern in Sledge's eyes. She pressed her lips together and glanced out towards the window for a second. Speaking from the heart, she replied,

"Sometimes it's better not to know, mate."

Seeing him in a disorientated state reminded Sledge of her previous experiences awaking in similar circumstances of the unknown. Due to her numerous traumas and the uninhabitable living conditions of the harbour, Sledge suffered severe insomnia.

"Where am I?"Max asked, trying to get his eyes to adapt to the light. Sledge's voice took a less compassionate tone, curtly answering,

"You're in the Shag-Pile mate. The £20 next to you is yours. Candy-Shilling said to go and see him."

Max got to his feet, gradually piecing together what happened. After he had been knocked out, Candy-Shilling had his body dragged into the Shag-Pile so he could pay off his debt. Furthermore, the vindictive gangster had left him a £20 cut so he could keep him addicted to his product, thus leveraging Max, like everyone else in his territory.

Tears emerged from the distressed young man's eyes as the realisation of how tragic his life had become. He wanted to be angry, but he hadn't the energy. He wanted to be sad, but he felt too numb. Max had no idea what he could do.

However, in that moment he made himself a promise. No matter how much his body craved the high he had been chasing, in that moment, Max found the drive to resist the power it had over him.

Taking a few seconds to compose himself, Max grabbed the £20 note and staggered back up to his feet. Slowly and steadily, he started to make his way to the door.

Sledge looked at him in shock,

"Where the hell do you think you're going?"

Max evasively answered he was going to see Candy-Shilling.

Sledge sharply replied,

"At this time? It must be about 6 in the morning! Here drink some of this before you do anything stupid."

Sledge retrieved a bottle of water from her cardigan pocket and gave it to Max.

After quickly drinking the water he continued out of the broken doorway, past all of the other fallen junkies. Sledge exclaimed sharply to herself,

"What a melt, he's going to end up dead."

Max gingerly made his way down the pathway towards Candy-Shilling's office with the £20 note in his hand.

His other hand reached into his hoodie pocket, tightly gripping his shiv. Part of him wanted to go and stick it in Candy-Shilling. But his body was bruised and his energy levels were dangerously low. He weakly dropped it on the litter filled cobbles by his feet. Though his body was in a fragile state, it lit a fire within him to leave the harbour once and for all.

Sledge left the Shag-Pile and lit up another cigarette, watching him with bated breath.

The newly determined young man continued on his journey, walking straight past Candy-Shilling's building without hesitation. Finally, he made it to the hole in the fence, leaving the hellish confines of the harbour. A subtle but genuine smile snuck across Sledge's face; at the sight of the young man leaving the area, for what she hoped would be the last time.

Once he had left the hellish confines of the harbour, Max felt a brief moment of joy. However, despite the colossal change he had achieved, it was short lived. His body was reeling from the physical abuse it had been subjected to. His head throbbed with pain. It was difficult to tell if these symptoms were being caused by the withdrawal of his addiction, or the effects of being knocked unconscious for several hours. Disorientated, he staggered over the street to the "Rough Tide Pub". Unsurprisingly, the pub was closed at that time in the morning.

Max took, what felt like a moment, to compose himself in his dazed state. In reality he was leant against the wall in a trance for around 25 minutes. Breathing deeply, he continued to stagger gingerly down the street.

Although he was unsure where he was going, the fact he was getting further away from the harbour, meant it was the right direction. He wandered aimlessly at a slow and painful pace.

As the weather swiftly changed from glaring sunlight to overcast, Max's body started to register the multiple traumas it had endured over the space of the past couple of days. His entire body started to ache; every step caused him excruciating pain.

Eventually, he started to recognise some of his surroundings. His uncoordinated, pilgrimage had brought him to the South-Side shopping precinct. Although it had been years since he had been in the precinct, he instantly recognised the Cutting Craft hardware store. A number of the other shops in the area had closed down or changed since his last visit. In his dazed state, Max's subconscious drew him to the familiarity of the shop.

He drew nearer to it as the shop began to open up. Before his path of self-destruction had ensued, Max remembered the generous, elderly man named Arthur, who had ran the shop for years. Cutting Craft was just opening and he hoped Arthur would help him in his hour of need.

Alas, this was not the case.

While Max was being consumed by his habits, Arthur was about to be bought out and replaced by a man named Bill McCray in a month's time.

Unfortunately, when he arrived at the shop, Mr McCray was outside observing the staff opening the store. Unlike his predecessor, Bill had nothing but distain for Max. As the desperate young man drew closer to the shopfront, an increasingly intensifying expression of disgust emerged on Mr McCray's face.

Fighting the violent physical effects his body was enduring, Max tried to ask for help.

Before he could utter a single word, Bill tutted loudly and sharply intervened in his northern accent,

"Oh just, clear off!"

Max was still trying to process his thoughts and convey his responses to plead his case. Once again he was interrupted by the curtly apathetic new store manager,

"For goodness sake, what a disgrace! It's not even nine o'clock in the bloody morning and you're staggering around high as a kite. I don't know what kind of a soup kitchen Arthur is running here, but I'm taking over soon and things are going to change. Now for the last time get away from my shop before you scare the customers off!"

Tears started to form in Max's eyes, Bill continued

"Go on, you're lucky I don't ring the police."

After enduring the manager's verbal onslaught, he left the area.

Although he was physically getting further away from the shop, every word of the manager's judgemental tirade echoed around his skull. Once again, Max was unaware of where his injured body was taking him. One of the few saving graces was that his fractured state of mind seemed to numb the physical pain of his wounded leg. But, the more the manager's words haunted his potentially concussed mind, the more he started to remember one of the teachers in his primary school.

Subsequently, he was mentally taken back to a vivid memory during his time in St Andrew's Primary School. Max was 8 at the time. He was irritated at Toby Kenny for spitting in his custard pudding during lunch break. Toby was academically very bright and always one of the teacher's favourite pupils.

However, he had recently developed a habit of slyly doing spiteful things, behind the teachers' backs.

He had started to realise that his reputation afforded him leverage over some of the other students. The opportunity had presented itself because there were no other witnesses at the table. Not to mention, it was almost impossible to prove after Toby had stirred the custard, while Max was attempting to tell the Dinner Ladies. Although his callous crime spree was thwarted at a later date, the child was unaware of the impact this one set of events would have on Max's life and future.

Once the third and final break of the day came, Max was still irritated at Toby's Lunchtime antics. At first he tried to take his mind off of it by playing with some of the other children. However, he caught a glimpse of Toby teasing another child near the staffroom. Max felt his body fill with a heated rage; he grabbed a stone and threw it at Toby.

Fortunately it missed. Unfortunately, it smashed through the staffroom window and destroyed a collection of teacups on the table. Soon after, a hoard of angry teachers spilled out into the playground looking for the culprit. Max was identified by one of the other students and promptly frogmarched to the headmaster's office.

Entering the receptionist's room, outside the office, each second dragged. He experienced a constant sinking feeling deep within his stomach.

It was a feeling of guilt, anger and sorrow; a daunting concoction for a child to bear. Max remembered the scent of coffee and biscuits flowing through the room as clearly as he did the burning aura of distain from the receptionists.

Suddenly, he heard a male voice rising in anger, booming through the closed pine door,

"What?! That's unbelievable! Send him in here at once!"
The door swung open, revealing the headmaster's face

21

glowing like an enraged blister. Max was ushered into the room. He tried to plead his case, but it was to no avail. The headmaster roared:

"For goodness sake Atkins, what a disgrace you are! It's no wonder your father left if you behave like this."

The words echoed in his mind, louder than before. All of a sudden, Max awoke from his trance and became aware of his new surroundings. While his mind had taken him to a repressed memory, his wounded body had taken him away from the shopping precinct towards city centre.

He found himself caught in a narrow path between two brick walls. The graffiti stained walls blurred as he staggered down the constricting pathway. Unbeknown to Max, he had entered a series of alleys leading to the Town Square.

At this point, it was nearing 10 o'clock. The rest of the city had come to life. As Max continued to struggle through the physical and psychological labyrinth, a man and his son were making their way down the alley from the opposite direction.

The dutiful father was hurriedly taking his child to primary school following a doctor's appointment.

"Why are we going down here Dad? Can't we go down to the beach instead?"

His son asked, sneakily hoping for a few extra hours of freedom. The boy's father answered;

"Don't be silly son; you've missed enough school as it is. If we hurry up you might make first break."

While the boy began to protest, they drew nearer to Max. The father stopped sharply and instinctively pulled his son behind him. Still staggering and feeling his way across the wall, Max's bloodshot eyes met theirs.

The father instantly grabbed his son's arm and swiftly took them back the way they came.

"Who was that?" The confused boy asked.

"A good reason to stay in school. Oh, sod this, we're getting a taxi". His father abruptly replied.

Following their retreat, Max was still in the alley venturing through his own personal hell. The suppressed internal wounds of his father leaving and the blame his inner child clung to, continued to torment him.

Witnessing the man's face fill with both fear and disgust only strengthened the demons that were clawing their way through Max's mind.

Once again in psychosis, he envisioned the man as his own father dragging his 8 year old self away from the monster he had become and leaving him in the hell he had created for himself.

All of a sudden, Max was hit with a sobering moment of clarity. He broke down and wept. From the age of 8, feelings of guilt and self-blame for his father abandoning his family had grown in his subconscious. Still caught in the clutches of physical injury, withdraw symptoms and a potential concussion, Max was unable to effectively process the magnitude of his discovery.

However, it resonated enough with him to enable him to continue his journey. He persevered on through the alley. Limping out into the Town Square, Max peered out at the passing public. Everyone appeared distant and preoccupied. Max's clarity allowed him to gauge people's expressions. Although most of them were too busy to notice him, it was obvious that the people who did felt uncomfortable.

Unsure of where to look, Max started to focus on where to go next. The sky was still overcast and dull, offering protection from the glare of the sun, but, it added to the bleakness of the atmosphere.

Filled with uncertainty and only £20 to his name Max looked to the ground and sighed in despair.

He started walking again. Subconsciously, movement felt more comfortable; when he stopped the hopelessness of his situation hit him harder. Continuing to look down as he walked his pace and breathing quickened with every negative thought that swirled in his head.

Suddenly, he saw a pair of brown shoes come into his line of sight. Grinding his movement to a halt, Max instinctively looked up, instantly recognising the man wearing them.

It was his former tutor, Fred Smith.

"Max?"

He exclaimed with shock and concern across his face, analysing the immense changes to the bright young student he once knew.

CHAPTER 3: CONSUMED

Overwhelmed at the sight of his former tutor and the first sign of genuine care anyone had shown for his wellbeing, Max felt his throat clamp up and his eyes water. Unable to speak, his gaunt face reddened, desperately attempting to contain the flood of emotions.

Fred put his hand on his former student's shoulder and gently suggested,

"Shall we go back to my flat and take a look at that leg? It's not far."

Max nodded, still intensely trying to hold back his emotions.

"No! Don't give him any money; these down and outs are confidence artists." An articulate, well-dressed man exclaimed, looking on from a few feet away. Fred's eyes burned with annoyance as his head swiftly turned to the man, simply replying,

"Thank you for your concern."

Though Fred's reply was courteous, his sharp delivery caused the onlooker to quickly retreat. As they made their way towards his flat, Fred tried to distract Max from the man's comments.

"My flat is just on the other side of Penelope Park, I can make you some breakfast if you want?"

Max finally managed to muster a sentence, fighting his tears with each word,

"I'm not trying to get any money… I just… don't know what to do…"

Fred softly replied,

"I know you're not. He shouldn't have dropped an opinion like that on the street, but, like all droppings on the street we need to wipe it off and move on."

Max laughed, grateful for the much needed levity. With Fred's assistance, they slowly but surely travelled through Penelope Park, eventually Fred's flat came into view. The throbbing physical pain and mental numbness interlocked, seemingly with each step. But, the closer they got to the flat, the safer he felt. Fred made light conversation as they walked, however, Max drifted in and out, unable to fully hear what he was saying.

Once they approached the entrance to the building, Max leant against the wall, while Fred readied his keys. Max was about to look back around the park, but, the sunlight was too bright. Cradling his head in his arms he leant against the wall.

Fred had almost got the door open, when a familiar American voice greeted him,

"Morning Fred."

It was his neighbour Lenny, who was out in his garden in his wheelchair. Lenny was a friendly but overbearing man. Once he noticed Max he commented

"Oh wow, looks like it's not a great day to be your buddy here. Must have been some party last night huh kid?"

Fearful of the effects Lenny's intrusive, high speed conversation may have on Max, Fred quickly interjected,

"Good morning Lenny, he's not feeling well today. Hopefully we can all get to know each other better at a later date. I don't think today's the day though."

With that, he ushered Max into the building. The

staircase had a wooden banister and smelt of lemon scented polish. Guiding Max towards the lift to his first floor flat Fred tapped the button. The metal lift door slid open, revealing a mirror. All of a sudden, Max felt a sickening feeling in his stomach, as if he had been punched. He barely recognised the mentally haunted and battle worn shell staring back at him. As he looked into the lift, it felt as though he was seeing a visual representation of the prison his life had become; a lonely box with no escape, a void of numbness with a tortured soul at the centre of it.

"Come on; let's get you home and have a look at that ankle." Fred gently encouraged, sensing Max's unease at seeing himself. The pair entered the lift and made it into the flat.

Upon opening the door, a familiar scent emitted from the flat. Max felt a rush of nostalgia from attending Fred's counselling classes at the University of Rockshore. While Max was taking in the atmosphere of his new surroundings, his mentor had put the kettle on. Max felt his heart beat increasing.

Before he knew it, he had run out of the flat, down the stairs and out of the building. He caught a glimpse of Lenny and sprinted through the gates, leaving the park. Periodically drifting out of conscious awareness, Max was unable to keep up mentally with where his body was taking him. One moment he was leaving Penelope Park, the next he was getting off a bus at Kingsport Harbour, which was outside of the city.

Following another hazy spell of dizziness, Max found himself at the Jolly Roger's Play Boat, an indoor play centre for children. Max had many happy memories at the venue. As he stood outside the entrance, he started to wonder if it was still the same inside. Hovering nervously, his eyes darted around the area, searching for onlookers.

To his surprise, the area was completely clear of people. He felt anxious. He knew that a man of his age hanging around a children's play area, may seem sinister to the general public, especially in his current condition. But, at the same time, something within him was telling him to go inside. Cautiously edging towards the entrance, Max noticed that nobody was in the admission kiosk. Nervously looking around once more, he entered the building. As soon as he entered the familiar smell of disinfectant and vacuum cleaned carpets entered his nose.

It felt as if he had been mentally transported back to his childhood. He was hit with a rush of nostalgia which filled him with excitement. His inner child's muscle memory kicked in and before he knew it, he was racing up the plastic rimmed stairs toward the facility. As he ascended the stairs, a middle aged female member of staff approached him. He instantly recognised the striped polo shirt with the Jolly Roger logo on the chest and arms of the shirt. To his surprise, she smiled at him and commented,

"Someone's keen, go ahead and enjoy yourself."

After a couple of seconds, Max realised that the same woman had said that to him before his 8th Birthday party. By the time he had made the recollection, he was at the top of the stairs. He turned back to face her, however, she was gone. He started to feel dizzy as he looked down, the light peering through the entrance door made him feel uneasy. Slowly turning back, he regained his balance and continued on into the play centre. Luckily, there was still nobody around. Passing the shoe station, where the kids would take off their shoes before entering, he noticed the compartments were all empty. He contemplated taking his own shoes off, but, suddenly he became distracted.

He instantly recognised the giant play boat before him, surrounded by blue foam mats painted to look like the ocean. The boat was exactly as he remembered it; three ropes dangled on each side for children to climb, padded ramps and a tunnel for people to enter. Inside of the boat, the ground floor tunnel led to a blue ball pond with sponge sea creature toys.

The upper deck had a maze of foam obstacles and a plank which the older children could jump off onto a large air bed leading to a bouncy castle, on the other side of the boat.

While Max admired the boat, the light from the window caught his eye. He started to notice a damp black mould around the windows and on the ceiling. He turned back to look at the boat, it was still painted just how he remembered it as a child. Cartoon style planks of wood with the "Jolly Roger" printed in black and white comic text on each side.

He looked round to the corridor where the toilets were located. To his horror, it was covered in black mould. It appeared as if it was growing into a black and white fungus in some areas.

The scent of disinfectant was still in the air. He couldn't understand how it smelt so clean and looked so disgusting. Suddenly, he heard the sound of someone mopping in the toilets. He froze with fear, if he was discovered loitering in the children's play area, the implications and consequences could be severe. Pulling himself together he turned to face the exit.

A man was there with his back to Max, he looked familiar, but he couldn't quite tell who it was. The area where the man stood was covered in the mould, it looked as though the man was investigating it. In a moment of panic he turned back to the boat, with the intention of hiding until the coast was clear. As he turned around, he felt an intense rush of panic shoot across his chest. Fred Smith stood before him, between him and the boat. Max had no idea how Fred had found him there. All of a sudden, the lost and bewildered young man noticed the crippling sorrow and fear upon his mentor's face. Fred's eyes watered and his lips quivered, in all the years Max had known his tutor, he had never shown such intense emotions. Before Max could talk, Fred pointed behind

Max and tearfully exclaimed,

"You need to fight it, and you need to survive! You're far too young and far too brilliant to let it consume you."

Stunned at Fred's intense emotions and seemingly cryptic advice, Max turned back around to the exit. Before him stood his mother, his sister and the man, who he now recognised to be his father. His father had neared the exit. He started to notice that there was a mass of mould bubbling and simmering in front of his mother and sister, they were facing him but had blank, emotionless expressions on their faces. His father was drifting further away and the bubbling mass of mould started to take shape. Black and white, rotten shards sprouted from the sides and a large orb like pod emerged pulsing from the centre of the mass.

It seemed to be expanding faster than his eyes could register. Before he knew it, the bulbous fungus before his eyes had grown to such a size that it visually dominated the room.

It had expanded to 20 feet tall, while the black and white rotting pod seemed to have stopped growing, the shards surrounding it continued to branch out around the room, they resembled crooked tentacles reaching for life. Max desperately wanted to move, but he was now paralysed with fear. He tried to prize his senses back to his mother and sister. But, before he could fully focus on them, the anxiety inducing sound of cracking glass could be heard. His attentions were turned back to the colossal growth, the source of the noise. Cracks appeared to slither across the face of the pod. The sound intensified with each jagged crack travelling across the pod. Still frozen in fear Max looked back to his family, he frantically looked back and forth between his sister and mother desperately hoping they would be able to escape.

His father had been eclipsed by the evolving monster. All of a sudden, the sound of breaking glass became excruciatingly loud. Dirty metallic needles had pierced through its rotten black and white face, forming a mouth. Simultaneously, similar needles protruded through the tentacles which now violently flared around the room. The gargantuan horror had finally taken its full form, resembling a twisted combination of a crack pipe and a Venus flytrap.

There it stood, an all-consuming monster that would destroy all in its path. Its vine like tentacles tore into Max's mother and sister, their faces still motionless, as the tentacles ripped through them and towards him.

Powerless to both his fear and the hellish situation he found himself in; Max helplessly quivered as the monster's needles pierced his wounded ankle. Desperately looking down, still frozen in horror, the vine like needles increased in size, rusting and oozing puss as they extended between his legs. Eventually they sharply punctured his anus and dragged him across the floor at speed, towards its jagged gaping mouth...

CHAPTER 4:
ASSESS AND REPAIR

"Max! Max? Oh thank goodness!" Fred exclaimed, visibly panting in relief.

Max frantically searched his surroundings, his eyes almost bulging out of his head and his body soaked with sweat as he gasped for breath. Once he had come to, he realised he was laid up on Fred's green sofa. Fred was perched on the coffee table by Max's side and visibly shaken by the condition of his once brilliant student. He gently commented,

"Welcome back. Are you alright?"

"Yeah, I'm, I'm better than I was. What happened to me?" he gingerly replied.

"All I can tell you… is one minute you were pacing around the room, talking about some sort of crime ring in South Town Harbour and the next minute your eyes rolled in the back of your head and you passed out and threw up."

Fred answered in concern and confusion.

Max looked down to the floor beside him, there was several sheets of kitchen roll, evidence of vomit and a spray bottle of disinfectant. Sighing in relief, Max leaned back on the sofa and looked up to the ceiling, where he saw a patch of damp mould. The sight of it made him short of breath, quickly turning back to Fred.

"Easy, easy, try not to move suddenly Max." Fred softly exclaimed, placing his hands gently on Max's shoulders. Fred made eye contact and added

"Now, there's an ambulance on the way, but, I'm not sure how long it will take to get here."

The troubled young man cradled his head in his hand,

"It's difficult to keep track of which nightmares are real and which ones aren't." He sighed.

Fred jokingly reassured him,

"Well, what you spewed on the floor was definitely real! The rest we can piece together as we go."

Realising that their time together may be limited, the traumatised young man felt a sudden urgency to talk to Fred. He felt a sense of desperation to rebuild his life. The feeling was so intense; it shifted his mind into a state of clarity.

"Fred, I need help. A lot of horrible and unbelievable things have been going on. The only thing I can tell you for certain is… I'm an addict."

Before he knew it, tears started to emerge from Max's eyes as he realised what he had just admitted. Fighting the ball of tension in his throat, he continued with a broken voice,

"I haven't seen my family in over a year and I've been living in a wasteland for months. But, I can't change anything for the better until I get my addiction under control."

Following Max's disclosures, Fred paused while soulfully maintaining eye contact. He had heard Max; however, he also understood the power of what he had just heard. In sitting with the silence, it allowed the wounded soul before him to hear himself and process the power of admitting his addiction.

"I think you know that what you have just admitted can take a lot of work. There's a lot of work ahead and it's going to be a battle and one which should not be faced alone. That being said you've just made a very powerful step in the right direction and I will do everything in my power to ensure that you won't have to face it alone."

Taking in Fred's words, Max nodded his head in reflection. During his time as a trainee counsellor, Max had been briefly introduced to the basic principles of addiction. But, now he was experiencing it from the other side. He realised he had layers of trauma to work through. Fred could sense that his former protégé was fearful of the daunting journey ahead of him. He gently interjected,

"While you were unconscious, I noticed the dried blood on the back of your head. Can you remember what happened?"

Max's mind flashed between the grotesque monster he had faced in his subconscious state and fragmented memories of the fight he had back at South Town Harbour. Tears re-emerged from his eyes. Initially he felt uneasy about his inability to recollect anything before or after the fight. However, as his fragile mind continued to work, he became haunted by distorted memories of his body being violated during his state of unconsciousness. Instantaneously, Max turned pale and begun to retch. Fred swooped in with a well timed bucket. As his former student spewed into the bucket, Fred knew he was showing all the signs of a concussion. However, even with all of his experience as a counsellor, he was unable to tell the full extent of Max's trauma.

Once he finished throwing up, Fred passed him a bottle of water. It was a litre bottle, but Max drank as much as he could. After gulping down all he was able to, he gasped for breath. It was as if he was trying desperately to wash down his feelings. Fred sensed that there was a lot he didn't know. However, he also realised that their time together before the ambulance got there was limited. Furthermore, he knew it was possible that he may pass out again. Suddenly Max cried out in despair

"My life is in ruins!" Thinking quickly Fred responded,

"I hear your pain, but at the same point, there is still life in the ruins."

He paused for a second, allowing Max to re-establish eye contact, before continuing…

"I know things seem hopeless. I also have no doubt that you are capable of turning it all around."

Fred could tell that his words had reached Max. While he still had his attention, he explained,

"Now Max, I understand that you've been through a lot, but in case you slip out of consciousness again, it's extremely important that we establish what's in your system. You mentioned that you were an addict. In terms of therapy, addictions are quite similar in nature. But, to ensure you have the best treatment, the less they have to guess, the better."

Max disclosed his drug of choice and explained that he hadn't been able to take it for a couple of days. However, he chose not to disclose what had happened to him in the Shag Pile. All of a sudden, they were interrupted by a loud ringing sound. Fred sprung to his feet, encouraging his injured guest to stay seated. As he suspected it was the ambulance responders. They swiftly entered the flat and attended to Max,

"Good morning, what's your name?" the first responder asked in a jovial but clear tone.

Once Max answered, the responder continued to ask a series of questions about the nature of his head injury and where he lived. He answered the questions as truthfully as he could, however, the responders' entrance and the subsequent change of atmosphere, started to affect Max. He felt his head start to spin again. During one of his answers, he puked up into Fred's bucket once more.

"Oh dear, looks like you owe this man a new bucket." The responder joked.

Once Max had finished he placed the bucket on the floor. He glanced at the responder with a confused look upon his face. Turning back to Fred, he started to say something before his eyes rolled in the back of his head and he fell unconscious once more.

When Max finally came to, he found himself awaking in a hospital bed. His eyes briefly opened, but, he hadn't the energy to keep them open. Although he couldn't keep his eyes open, he became aware of continuous humming sounds coming from machinery noises around the area. Every so often beeping could be heard. For the first time he could remember, Max felt relaxed. It felt as though he was wrapped in a marshmallow, he had almost forgotten the sensation of a soft, clean pillow behind his head. He started to move his fingers, caressing the thin cotton sheet which covered him. Contented with his surroundings, he noticed his arm had been hooked up to a drip feed. Inhaling deeply he turned his head; he saw there was a note with his name in large handwritten letters by his bedside.

Max attempted to roll over to his side. As he turned, he winced and exhaled in pain. It had become apparent that his lower back and hips were throbbing with pain. Despite the moderate physical pain he felt in moving, Max was still feeling better than he had felt in recent memory. Enduring the strain, he stretched over and reached the note.

"Ah, look who's up then." A nurse commented as she came over to check on him.

Max twisted back to a neutral position, still wincing in pain, his note in hand. Before he could read the note, the nurse added,

"I wouldn't move around too much at the moment, get some rest love. I'll go and inform the doctor you're awake. Oh, I see you've found your friend's note. He was here for hours; he only just left about half an hour ago, 'said he'd be back tomorrow, poor man looked exhausted."

By the time she had finished her sentence, the nurse had already made haste. Max unfolded the paper, the note read,

"Dear Max,

I am sorry I am unable to be with you when you awaken. Sadly, time and age have caught up with me (it has turned out to be quite a day)

However you are feeling when you awaken, I want you to know that you are not alone on this journey. You may feel obligated to beat the addiction by yourself. But, your chances of success are more likely with professional help.

I will catch up with you tomorrow.

P.S. If you are discharged beforehand, please get a taxi to Cabot Court and I will cover the cost."

Once Max had finished reading Fred's letter, he noticed a doctor approaching in his peripheral vision. The doctor closed the curtain around the bed and introduced himself,

"Hello Mr Atkins, I'm Dr Beverly. How are you feeling?" Max, who was still coming to and heavily influenced by the pain killers which were being pumped into his body: explained that he was feeling good, apart from the pain in his lower back and hip when he moved. Dr Beverly maintained a professional tone and stated

"Mr Atkins, we've noticed a number of injuries on your body. We've got you hooked up to a drip to keep you hydrated. We've also taken some blood samples. The results suggest you are severely malnourished and there are traces of stimulants. Now you're awake, we'd like to keep you in over night to examine the full extent of your injuries and how we can best treat them."

Taken aback by the information that was relayed to him and the timeframe in which they wanted him to stay, Max asked,

"What time is it now?"

Dr Beverly looked at his watch and told him it was 19:35 at night.

Meanwhile, Fred had just arrived back home at his Cabot Court Flat by Penelope Park. As he entered, he was hit by the pungent stench of disinfectant and putrid stomach acid. Fred held a handkerchief to his mouth and nose through fear of gagging. Making haste, he turned the lights on and opened as many windows as he could. He took a few deep breaths of fresh night air through the open window. The city caught his eye, the street lights glowed and the skyline blinked with lights coming on. The sky a calming combination of peach, purple and light blue as the sun was setting. Following his brief moment of tranquillity, he was ready to cleanse his home from vomit.

Taking one last gasp of fresh air, he rolled up his shirt sleeves and began his task. Usually, cleaning offered an opportunity to mentally escape from life's worries, but on this occasion it was more difficult. The odour of vomit, mixed with disinfectant, combined with the stains upon his laminated flooring; continued to haunt him. It was as if his mind was imprisoned by the memory of Max collapsing. He vividly recalled Max pacing around and describing South Town Harbour as a hellish wasteland before passing out. The feelings of shock and powerlessness resurfaced within Fred, still uncertain of how much truth there was to what he had heard. The only aspect he did know to be true was the physical pain and psychological suffering that Max had endured due to his addiction.

Once he had finished cleaning, a sharp twinging sensation throbbed through Fred's shoulder. In assisting

Max through the park and up into his flat and intensely scrubbing his laminated floor, he had pulled a muscle in his shoulder. It started to become apparent that the day had taken a physical and mental toll on him. The dull ache continued to throb and his mind continued to race. He got up off the floor and sat on his sofa, as he sat there he became short of breath and felt tightness in his chest. All of a sudden, he became anxious and bombarded with seemingly trivial, yet intense internalised questions. What if Max needed more physical assistance tomorrow? How could he continue to clean the flat? Would he be able to get a good night's sleep with his shoulder injury? The more he dwelled on his anxieties, the more intense and upsetting the questioning became.

He started to cross-examine himself. Similarly to the plant like monster in Max's state of unconsciousness, Fred too, found himself being internally consumed. An onslaught of personal attacks and existential questions echoed around his mind, each one louder than the last.

"If only I had seen this coming years ago. Decades of experience and I still couldn't do anything to help prevent his downfall. Is he too far gone to come back? How many other lives have been destroyed under my watch?"

Staring deeply into space, the black hole in his mind consumed all the positive matter in his head.

Fred's eyes fixated onto his beige walls. Eventually the negative voices quietened, but he was still left with a sinking feeling of negativity. Trapped in a numbed state of despair, it felt as though part of him had travelled somewhere else.

Gradually the ticking from his kitchen clock became more noticeable. Although it was a minor distraction it was just enough to bring him back into conscious awareness. Fred recognised his negative thought process from an external perspective.

It felt as though he was trapped under water and desperately battling for air, urgently trying to swim to the surface. He began to take steps to bring himself out of it, focusing on his breathing before closing his eyes. After a few moments he started to feel slightly more at ease. Upon opening his eyes, it felt like he had recalibrated his mind back into the present moment. During his lifetime, Fred had endured and persevered through countless bouts of hopelessness, anxiety and depression. Although it had been quite some time since he last experienced it, the feelings were as intense as ever, but so was his resolve.

Once Fred managed to break the negative cycle, he found that he was able to build upon the momentum of positivity within him. Now Fred had been freed from his torment, everything looked less bleak. He glanced over at the clock on the kitchen wall.

"I'd better call Raymond before the night escapes me" he thought to himself, before reaching over to his telephone. Raymond was another protégé of Fred's. He worked as a counsellor at the University of Rockshore, offering support to the daytime students. Although Fred was his mentor, Raymond was an experienced counsellor in his own right. He had worked with a range of different clients for over a decade and a half. Their relationship was both personal and professional, having first met during Raymond's teenage years.

Fred still vividly remembered Raymond as a black teen, living in "Jacksville", an area notorious for antisocial behaviour and nationalistic views. When Fred first knew him, he was at odds with another Jacksville boy named Steve, who attended the same school. Fred knew Steve's father from the "Town Cryer" pub where they would drink together.

One afternoon, Fred was returning home to his Cabot Court flat when he saw a commotion unfold in Penelope Park. The two boys were brawling, surrounded by other adolescents goading them to continue, cheering for blood. Both Raymond and Steve were bruised and bloodied. Fred quickly intervened, shouting,

"All right you lot, I've just phoned the police! You two stop fighting and stay there. The rest of you clear off."

The onlookers of the group promptly left the scene, some of them shouted abuse and stuck their fingers up, but they all left accordingly. Raymond and Steve looked to be in a standoff. They had stopped fighting and were breathing heavily, but they still had their fists up, neither of them trusted the other enough to put their hands down. Fred calmly invited them to sit with him on a park bench. He sat between them and explained

"Now we've got the riff raff out of the way and fight is over, perhaps we can talk?" Both of the lads remained silent, caught in a dilemma of fear and rage.

He didn't tell them that he hadn't actually called the police, but, gradually Fred managed to help work through their anger and calm them down. Once the conflict had been reduced he sent them home in different directions.

As a frustrated teenager, trying to find his way in the world, Raymond felt inspired by what he had seen Fred accomplish. From that day, he would greet Fred when he saw him in passing. As the years went on, Raymond would sometimes stop to chat and share his feelings. Eventually, their rapport developed and Raymond became inspired to pursue counselling as a vocation. Reliving months of memories within seconds, Fred came to and began to input his number, twisting the rotary dial on his beige 1970's telephone.

"Fred, what do I owe the pleasure?"

"Hello Raymond, I'm sorry to trouble you. I'm wondering if you could do me a favour?"

"Sure, what's been going on?"

"Do you remember that student I used to teach who went missing a couple of years ago?"

"Yes, yes Max wasn't it? I remember it affected you quite a lot when he suddenly left the Uni."

"I've found him Raymond…"

Fred's voice started to tremble with emotion as he

43

explained what had happened to Max. Although he was reluctant to accept the responsibilities that it would entail, Raymond could hear the vulnerability in his mentor's voice. If anyone else had asked him to do it, he would have most likely refused. But, Fred was very important to him. He often referred to him as "a cornerstone in the foundation of his life".

He reassured Fred that he would do everything he could to support the young man through his rehabilitation.

"Thank you my friend, it means more than you know. Turns out I'm not as young as I used to be."

"No worries Fred, we'll touch base tomorrow. Let me know if you need anything else."

Satisfied with the outcome of his phone call, Fred hung up and exhaled in relief. Sitting back in the sofa, he rested his hand on the seat next to him. To his surprise, something didn't feel right. The sofa still had a nasty odour to it, but the sweat stains had dried. On further inspection, Fred discovered that there was a dark patch where Max had been sitting. All of a sudden, he remembered when Max awoke screaming as he violently slid down the sofa.

Later that night, back at the hospital Max was starting to become more aware of the physical damage his body had endured, even with the painkillers that were being pumped into his arm.

Dr Beverly was keeping Max under observation due to his head injury. It felt like an eternity for him, if what he experienced in South Town Harbour was hell, this was purgatory. Fatigued and docile he sat in his bed; every so often the nurses would look in on him. Eventually, Dr Beverly returned and enquired about the pain in his hip. He closed his bedside curtain once again and asked

"Are you able to turn over?"

Max shuffled over allowing the doctor to assess the damage. Once he was in position, the doctor lifted the sheet cover. A concerned look emerged across the stoic doctor's face.

There was a patch of dried blood on the under sheet Max had been lying on, evidence of bleeding from his rectum. Dr Beverly's stoic expression wavered. Though he had not asked his patient, he strongly suspected that the injuries were the result of a sexual assault.

The concerned doctor reassured Max that his injuries could be treated, but he also enquired as to how the injuries occurred. As soon as he was asked, Max's mind flashed back to the monster's needle covered vines slithering towards him.

"I... just woke up with it." He answered, his voice shaking and the colour draining from his face.

"It's important that you know there are people you can talk to and if you wish to report to the police, our hospital can provide records, with your consent."

Max shook his head, frantically trying to fight his tears, before clearing his throat and enquiring about the medical procedure. It was clear that Max didn't want to face discussing his ordeal with Dr Beverly or the police. Dr Beverly couldn't help but feel sorrow and frustration. He realised that Max was a man and legally he had no right or power to take any further action.

However, in witnessing his reaction, it all but confirmed everything he feared and he too felt powerless. Nonetheless, he answered his patient's questions and maintained his professionalism. With the support of Dr Beverly and several other members of night staff at St Catherine's Hospital, Max made it through the night, once again drifting in and out of consciousness throughout.

The following morning he had all of his wounds and injuries tended to. He had also been provided with a clean hooded tracksuit from the St Catherine's Hospital Clothes Bank. Although his new clothing was clean, he still had to carry his old clothing in a carrier bag. The sight and smell of the clothing disgusted him. Physically he was on his way to recovering, but mentally, the journey was just beginning.

Within minutes of exiting the hospital a taxi swooped in

to collect him.

"Alright mate? Hop in, where you heading?"

The taxi driver enquired, rolling up his window as Max entered the backseat. Sliding across the leathery back seat Max instructed the driver to travel to Cabot Court. The driver glanced at him in his rear view mirror.

He contemplated making small talk with his passenger, however, he quickly decided against the notion. Max's eyes were glazed with sorrow. It looked as if his soul was travelling through a treacherous blizzard within his own mind.

The driver had already pulled out of the car park, just looking at his passenger made him want to complete the journey as quickly as possible. As they passed various business buildings in the outskirts of the city, Max's depressed mind contemplated the hopelessness of his life. He was determined to beat his addiction, devastated by the state he awoke in the previous day.

But no matter how good his intentions were, Max was unable to feel anything that resembled positive emotions. His body screamed for something it hadn't had in days. Jittering and rocking, Max felt hungry and unfulfilled in every imaginable sense. It felt like he didn't even deserve to exist. As their brief but harrowing journey progressed into the city, he saw a hooded figure, with their hands in their pockets, strutting down the street. As the figure faced the taxi, Max muttered

"Candy-Shilling's sent someone after us!"

"What's that mate?"

The driver replied in a less personable and more concerned tone than before.

Max put his hood up, sharply replying

"Just drive, it's fine, they might not have seen us."

The driver couldn't see anyone except for a few elderly people on the street. He silently continued driving, anxiously eager to get the young man to his destination.

"Why the hell is he sending people after me? I don't owe

him money anymore! Is he trying to have me killed?" Max thought to himself. He turned his head so he could peek out of his hood without revealing his face.

To his horror there were two other faceless hoodies searching the streets. Regardless of how irrational the hallucinations were, Max was convinced that their existence was reality. Once again he hid under his hood and put his hands in his pockets. Suddenly he felt the crispness of the twenty pound note in his pocket. As soon as he touched it, the idea of going back to the harbour and getting another fix entered his mind like a viral infection. The notion raised his heartbeat and temperature.

CHAPTER 5:
TOUCHING BASE

Meanwhile, Fred had just woken up. Having fallen into a deep sleep following his phone call with Raymond, he felt rested and ready to get to work in helping his former student. The flat was still faintly haunted by the aromas of the previous day, however, they were considerably less overbearing. Sitting at his table, he ate his breakfast which consisted of cereal, a selection of fruit and a pot of yoghurt.

Each morning, Fred would eat his breakfast watching live internet videos of the sun setting in different parts of the world. Although it was somewhat of an eccentric ritual, the sentiment that the day had ended somewhere else motivated Fred to make the most of his day, while he had the unguaranteed privilege of doing so. The birdsong emitting from Penelope Park provided a harmonious background noise, complimenting the taste of his first meal of the day. Although his shoulder still felt tender, Fred felt considerably better than he did the previous evening. Raymond was scheduled to arrive at his flat later that day, after he had finished seeing his clients at the

University.

Just as Fred finished his breakfast, the buzzer to his flat sounded.

"Fred! It's Max. I've already paid for the taxi, can you let me in?"

He was surprised as to how he had the means and why Max had paid, when he had offered to pay for it. Nonetheless, he let his recovering protégé in and eagerly awaited him in his door way. The lift door could be heard opening and shutting as Max made his ascension up to the flat. It took about a minute and a half for the lift to reach the first floor, but it felt a lot longer to Fred. When the door opened, Max came out, still worse for wear but in a hurry to enter the flat. He was also carrying two bags. A small paper chemist bag containing a mixture of medication prescribed at the hospital and the plastic bag for his dirty, battle worn clothing.

"How are you today Max?" Fred asked, trying to mask the concern in his voice he quickly added

"And how did you pay for that taxi?"

"I really appreciate you offering to pay for it, but I wanted to pay my own way." He paused for a second, his eyes glazed over with emotion.

"Besides, I had a £20 note that I really needed to get rid of." Fred sensed that there was a great deal of pain embedded below the surface of Max's last statement; nevertheless, he invited him in and did not press the subject any further.

Entering the flat for the second time in two days, the young man walked into the open plan living room. The faint aromas of disinfectant and vomit re-entered his nose. Though they were not as pungent as the previous day, Max's conscience amplified them and he felt an overwhelming sense of guilt.

"Cup of tea?" Fred asked, hoping to distract him from his thoughts. The troubled young man's gaze arose from the floor to answer. In a split second, his focus was drawn to the blood stain on Fred's sofa. Immediately his mind was drawn back to his injuries… and how they were caused. His voice shuddering, Max asked

"Actually, could… could I please have a bath or a shower? I don't want to impose… but I haven't had one in…"

"Of course you can, there's a fresh towel and an old tracksuit on top of the cupboard in there. Give me a shout if you need anything."

Max gingerly shuffled into the bathroom, biting his lip as the realisation of what had happened to him set in. Once he entered he closed the door and locked it. Finally able to release his tears, he held his breath trying to not to draw attention to his broken state. At that moment Fred turned on his kitchen radio. The anonymity the ambient noise provided enabled Max to fully express his pain. Leaning into the closed wooden door with his head cradled in his arms, he froze for a couple of minutes, letting his emotions wash over him.

Eventually, he pulled himself together and turned on the shower. The water pelted onto the alloy surface of the bath, as it echoed around the room Max started to feel safe enough to undress.

Although the clothes from the hospital were clean, he was happy to be freed from them. Climbing into the bath he stood under the warmth of the water. It took a few moments to get it to the right temperature; but after a while, the soothing sensation of the water cascading down his back, slowly started to ease his shock. His mind was finally enabled to drift to a less harrowing place. Blankly staring into the perspiring, cream ceramic tiles on Fred's wall, he felt a moment of quiet peace. Whether it was the medication the hospital had prescribed finally taking effect, or that he was finally beginning to adapt to the lack of substances; it was a sensation he had not experienced in several years.

Looking to the surface of the bath, he noticed the dark

earthy colour of the water streaming towards the plug hole. The visual representation of his dark past leaving his body felt cathartic. On the other side of the door Fred was respecting Max's privacy but also keeping an ear out for him and an eye on the clock, to ensure his safety. He was relieved when he heard the shower, he had had concerns about him passing out in the bath and drowning. Nonetheless, a short time later his tender guest re-emerged from the bathroom; visibly cleaner and slightly more relaxed as he re-entered the room.

"Cup of tea?" Fred asked again. Max subtly smiled, graciously accepting his host's offer.

Shuffling into the kitchen Fred flicked his kettle on and began preparing the tea,

"You take milk and sugar?"

"Yes… please." Fred was relieved; he wanted to make him a sweet tea because he believed it may help Max with the shock of his ordeal.

"Can I get you any breakfast? I've got cereal or I can cook you something."

"I don't want to put you to any trouble."

"Nonsense, it would be more reassuring to see you eat something to be honest. I'll do you a full English!"

He bowed his head and smiled at his host's enthusiasm, gently nodding in approval. Fred excitedly clapped his hands and rubbed them together

"Right then! Get this down you and I'll crack on."

The young man went to collect the fresh cup of tea before Fred added

"Have you ever tried it with a spot of honey in it?"

"Can't say I have" Max replied, with a slightly confused look upon his face,

"Sounds nice though."

With that Fred added some honey to his tea. After he had seasoned the tea, he proceeded to fry up the breakfast. Smells of cooking fat and grease filled the room. At first he was concerned that it may irritate his guest's gag reflexes again.

However, to their mutually pleasant surprise, the aroma of a freshly cooked breakfast revitalised Max. For almost a year he had been living off inedible scraps and shoplifted snacks. As he raised the cup to his lips, the steam from the hot tea entered his sinuses, creating condensation upon his nose. The scent of honey entered his nostrils while he gently blew it, attempting to cool it down. Slowly sipping the tea, Max felt his insides warm up. It wasn't long before breakfast was served. A full plate of baked beans, eggs, sausages, black pudding, bacon, fried tomato, mushroom and toast was placed in front of Max.

Fred knew that increased appetite, particularly for carbohydrates, was a common withdraw symptom from Max's drug of choice. He also knew that his guest may not be able to eat much of it, but he wanted to give him the option to eat as much as he wanted.

"Don't feel obliged to eat it all if you can't face it. Feel free to tuck in though; your body needs to rebuild its strength."

Max mumbled in agreement while eating his egg dipped sausage. After savouring several mouthfuls of food, he quickly remembered that Dr Beverly had given him an information leaflet about concussions. Excusing himself from the table, he quickly retrieved it from the bathroom and handed it to his host. When he sat down again, his body started to feel fatigued from his burst of energy. Fred glanced at the leaflet and observed Max. He understood that the information regarding his concussion was important. But, he also wondered if deep down it felt unnatural for Max to feel comfortable and he was looking for an excuse to leave.

"Ugh, I'm sorry Fred; I'm feeling kind of full at the moment. I'm going to have a break from it."

Max exclaimed, rubbing his forehead with the palm of his hand.

"That's fine mate, no worries."

Fred reassured his disorientated guest in a gentle tone, before informing him that Raymond would be coming round later in the day to meet him.

Max had never met Raymond before, he instantly felt nauseous. The prospect of meeting somebody new in his current state caused him to feel uneasy. He found himself wracked with shame, guilt and self-loathing; he needed to get out of the situation. Instantly noticing Max's hesitance, Fred explained,

"I understand you may feel uncomfortable about meeting new people; but Raymond is an experienced colleague and has been a friend of mine for a very long time. If we're going to get you through this, we're going to need his help. Now there's a facility that will help you fight the addiction, but we need to build a support network for you on top of that…"

Fred paused mid-sentence, recognising that the blood had drained from Max's already gaunt face. It was clear his focus had returned to his internal pain and he was unable to hear what Fred was saying. Max weakly uttered,

"I… I don't want to impose if you have someone coming over." Visibly squirming in his chair, he started to become short of breath. He quickly added,

"I can do this on my own. I need to! I got myself into this, I can bloody well get myself out of it!"

Fred calmly interjected

"I can hear that the idea of meeting someone new is very difficult for you at this time. It sounds like you're quite anxious and there are a lot of fears in your mind. I'm sensing there's a real pressure in your mind to take on this monster on your own, rather than let anyone else into your life at this time."

Max's dilated pupils rose to meet Fred's. Behind his haunted stare, his mind flashed back to the all-consuming, carnivorous monster that he saw during his subconscious terror. It's hellish mouth still gaping open, waiting to feed on him.

"I appreciate you've been through a lot and Raymond will understand if you need more time to rest."

"I've seen it! I've seen the monster; it looked like a giant mutated plant, only it was covered in scum, needles and decay. It took over the whole room!"

Confused and concerned, Fred asked

"This room?"

"No, it was at the Jolly Roger's play boat. It was over 20 feet tall and its' needles pierced through my leg and dragged me across the floor."

At first Fred suspected that the hallucination Max was describing was due to his concussion. But as the young man started to sob and struggle for breath, Fred began to realise that the events he was describing, coincided with his violent reactions while he regained consciousness the previous day. He was being re-triggered and it was causing him to have an anxiety attack. Despite the challenges his fragmented memory could present, Fred detected some very real emotional trauma at the core of Max's nightmare.

"Ok Max, I hear you. You need to breathe. This monster may be running rampant in your thoughts, but it doesn't exist in the here and now. Breath with me and come back to the here and now, it's where all the oxygen is."

While his former tutor guided him through some intense breathing exercises, Max felt the crippling tension start to ease with each gasp. It took a few moments for him to settle into the exercise, but once he did, the monster's hold over his body and mind gradually became less potent. As his pace calmed, his gasps slowed to steady breaths, enabling him to fully appreciate the sensation of oxygen entering his lungs.

After a few moments, Fred checked in with Max. Once they started talking Fred felt reassured that he was in a better place than he was a few moments prior. He realised that he was still tender, however, he wanted to allow Max some space to be heard. As they regained eye contact, Fred commented,

"That felt intense. I heard you were in a great deal of pain and anguish at the mental image of this monster. But, I'm also wondering if it's an advantage in some ways. As horrifying as it may be, it can be easier to defeat something if you can see it."

Max stared into the ground while he pondered in reflection. Observing his guest, Fred continued,

"It's interesting you described this monster as a mutated carnivorous plant. You know, I… I don't think you've lost your knack for counselling analogies."

Max's eyes arose from the ground, meeting Fred's, filled with inquisitive hope. Showing signs of the brilliant counselling student that Fred once knew, he started to make sense of the extreme subconscious terror he had experienced.

"I saw the monster of addiction, and it has grown from my pain."

Fred's face lit up, he excitedly exclaimed

"That's right! The pain is the seed which that monster has grown from. There may have been several aspects of your life that contributed to it, that you were unaware of, or even too afraid to face. But, they are the roots beneath this monstrosity. They are the addiction's power."

Max started to shake, listening to Fred's analysis filled him with hope and warmth. Yet he also felt vulnerable and concerned. For the first time he could remember, he didn't feel alone.

"It all started back at the university course. I remember this one night, I was walking home and I just felt inadequate. All of the other people in that course had suffered in some way. They all had life experience. I felt this awful void inside of me and I had no right to feel that way, because I'd had a sheltered life, living in a good home with a loving family."

"Everyone has a right to feel. If we didn't, we wouldn't be human."

Upon hearing Fred's response, Max picked up his cutlery

and resumed eating the substantial plate of food in front of him. Noticing that he'd regained his appetite, the seasoned counsellor continued,

"As humans we have a habit of quantifying and comparing things. But sometimes it isn't practical. When it comes to pain, it can be downright harmful. You were feeling this void in your life and you couldn't allow yourself to fully accept or express it, because you didn't feel you had the right to feel. Not only that, but you felt guilt for not suffering."

During Fred's reflection, he noticed Max's pace of eating had increased. He was unsure of whether his rapid consumption of the food, was because of his withdrawal symptoms, or a means of blocking out what he was hearing and coping with the re-emerging emotions.

"I'm wondering if you're still trying to fill that void now." After a few seconds, Fred's words sunk in. Max's rate of consumption slowed. The knife and fork clinked on the rims of the plate. He started to recognise how natural it felt to revert to coping mechanisms when faced with his own feelings. A silence fell upon them. Fred could sense that the gears were turning in Max's head. He was digesting what he had heard and he was able to see more of what was going on within himself.

He was reminded of the power of being heard; simply having someone to listen while he voiced his feelings without judgement had enabled his feelings to float to the surface of his awareness. While his mind was processing his thoughts, his eyes had veered to the walls. He had reached a moment of peace, no longer having to shovel food down his throat; he didn't feel the need to run from them anymore. Yet, he also knew that there were too many repressed feelings to unpack in one sitting. He had made a start and was content to sit in a comfortable silence. His thoughts progressed towards the rehabilitation centre that Fred had mentioned and what his journey towards recovery would entail.

He started to ask about the facility. Sipping his tea, Fred replied,

"We will get to that shortly. Firstly, how are things with your family? I know this may be painful, but before anything else, it's important to establish a network of people to support you."

Max's face instantaneously became filled with pain and discomfort,

"My mother and my sister are my only family. They don't ever want to see me again."

"Do you want to see them again?" Fred asked.

Although he remained silent, it was clear from the young man's face that he missed his family. Noticing his yearning for family, Fred continued,

"I wouldn't be surprised if they didn't feel the same way." Max started to feel uncomfortable and arose from his seat at the table. Once again, he found himself physically trying to escape his internal discomfort. Hesitating, he tried to stop himself from moving.

"Shall we move into the lounge?" Fred asked, attempting to alleviate some of the pressure.

Max nodded in acceptance of his invitation, he made his way over to the sofa. His fingers were trembling, showing signs of his body still trying to escape the immense pressure of his past. As they sat down Fred placed his hand over Max's,

"Don't forget to breathe, if this is too much for you at the moment, you're more than welcome to lay down and watch the telly."

Max's eyes darted to the large box television in the corner of the room, before resuming eye contact with Fred.

"Is that even in colour?"

"Yes, you cheeky sod." He replied in jest.

They started to chuckle, easing some of the tension. A few seconds after, as the smiles faded from both of their faces, Max felt a burning desire emerge within him to face the pain inside of him. Before he knew it, words flowed from his mouth and he was explaining everything.

"Everything went wrong during that counselling course. At the time, I told myself the best way to gain more life experience is to live it. If I could know what it was like to experience drugs, I'd instantly connect with potential clients that others may be scared of. So, I started hanging out with some people I probably shouldn't have, but we were there for each other. My mum didn't like them because she thought they were into drugs, mother knows best I guess, cause' they were. A few months down the line I started experimenting with different drugs with them. It started off small; my friend Misty shotgun kissed me with whacky baccy. Those were the good times.

After that I got a bit more adventurous, nothing too serious though, conversation starters and conversation stoppers. I was still in control. But then, I found out my father had died... I didn't know what to feel and whenever I did, I didn't want to. I didn't want the drugs anymore, but, I needed them. By this point I barely saw my mum or sister and when I did, we just clashed. Me and my friends were down South Town Harbour almost every night and day. Then Candy-Shilling gave me, 'a night I wouldn't forget' for free. I was hooked instantly. From that moment on my life became about chasing one of the most addictive drugs known to man."

Following Max's recollection Fred methodically responded,

"The potency of what you're addicted to can be extremely difficult to overcome. But, the underlying issue... the... the seed that's spawned this monster plant in your mind, that's often what leads to people's downfall, relapse and in exceptionally tragic cases, death. The physical cravings and psychological conditioning of the vice are challenging. But, they are more manageable if you can enhance your self-awareness and empathise with what has driven you to this point. Regardless of what you are addicted to, the internal feelings will be the defining factor.

That's why it is imperative that they are brought to light."

As he heard his mentor, he felt reassured that no matter how dark his days had been; there was hope that life could get better. It felt as though being reunited with Fred was a beacon of light, slowly guiding him through the dark waters of his past and the uncertainty of his future.

In the relatively short time they had been talking, it seemed that the more he opened up, the more he felt accepted.

Max wanted to continue exploring his past, but the effects of his condition caught up with him. He needed to rest. All of a sudden, he felt contentedly void of energy. It was a bizarre sensation, his body exhausted, yet his mind was free for the first time he could remember.

CHAPTER 6:
ROOTS

Later that day, Raymond had just finished with his final client at the University of Rockshore. Concluding the writing and storing of his paperwork, he took some time to sit in his room with a cup of tea. His thoughts had become dominated by Fred's phone call the previous night. Even though it was brief, Raymond could sense how deeply yesterday's events had affected Fred, from the emotion within his voice. He remembered how concerned his mentor was following Max's abrupt departure from the university.

Throughout their years working together, in various capacities, Raymond was one of the few people Fred felt comfortable enough to confide in.

Fred had earned a reputation for being an excellent counsellor throughout the Rockshore area. But, like a lot of counsellors, he preferred to listen to others and work through their problems, than to discuss his own. Raymond was of a similar nature. However, having known Fred since his adolescence, he was more attuned to picking up on his emotions.

In some ways Raymond was the closest thing to family Fred had left.

In his earlier years, Raymond would become irritated when he could sense something was wrong, but Fred would refuse to talk about it. He knew something wasn't right, yet he was powerless to do anything about it. However, as time went on and Raymond became more settled in his role as a professional counsellor, Fred would turn to him in moments of need. Even though their communication had evolved, the unspoken emotion Raymond heard in Fred's voice still echoed in Raymond's head. He knew he would just have to wait for Fred to address it at his own pace. But, in caring for him as much as he did, despite his years of experience, the frustrated teenager that wanted to help was still somewhere inside.

Finishing his tea he left his counselling room and navigated his way through the university. The rhythm of his footsteps steadily pacing across the smooth concrete corridor floor provided a welcome distraction from his concerns and baggage. Similarly to Fred the previous evening, a momentary change enabled him to refocus his mind. Before he knew it he was in the car park, entering his large grey estate car.

Once his mind had settled, Raymond was able to adopt a less emotionally driven way of looking at things. Rather than fixating on what Fred hadn't told him, he focused on what he had. He recalled Fred's admiration for Max's abilities to empathise with clients, despite not having any previous experience or qualifications. Raymond suspected that his mentor saw aspects of himself in the young man, thus feeling more responsible for his safety. Max was young for a trainee counsellor. Although the course was open to anyone over 18, there was a thorough vetting process for all potential candidates. Fred had disclosed to Raymond that he had vouched for the young man, but other tutors were unsure due to his age and lack of entry level certificates. It was only due to Fred's position as an experienced counsellor and senior member of staff, that Max was granted access to the course.

At the time Raymond affirmed his mentor's decision. He trusted Fred's judgement and knew that each student enrolled on the course was required to attend personal therapy, because of the sensitive nature of the work they were doing. When Fred initially discussed Max's tired demeanour, lack of attendance and eventual departure; Raymond questioned whether he was attending the private therapy sessions. It was common for people to drop out of counselling courses. But from what Raymond had heard, Max seemed to be suffering the effects of dramatic changes.

After a month of absence and numerous unsuccessful attempts to contact Max and his mother, who was his emergency contact, he was officially removed from the course. Following his removal, Fred personally tried to call Max at his home address. But, alas it was to no avail.

Max's mobile was cut off and when he contacted his mother, she refused to talk about him.

Naturally these occurrences raised more questions and concerns for Fred and intensified the feelings of guilt he carried.

Fred was still able to conduct himself as personably and professionally as he always had when working at the university and seeing private clients. But, Raymond could tell that it haunted him, which was painful for him to witness. It dawned on Raymond, that he understood Fred's feelings better than he had realised. The person he needed to be mindful of was Max. While he could empathise with his mentor's feelings, he had no idea what had led Max down the path of self destruction. All he knew for certain was that the young man would be feeling extremely vulnerable. After he had aligned his thoughts, Raymond phoned Fred.

Back at the flat Max had taken an afternoon nap. His body lay peacefully on Fred's spare bed, perfectly still apart from the gentle rhythm of his breath. However, while his battle worn body was silently recovering, his subconscious mind was once again processing the seemingly inscrutable origins of his pain. Once again he found himself at Jolly Roger's Play Boat, this time he was inside the boat.

He was in a cramped tunnel inside the boat's structure. As he shuffled his way forward he started to remember that it led to the foam obstacles on the top deck of the boat.

Eventually he reached the top. Before he could collect his thoughts a rustling sound captured his attention. It was a curious sound emitting from the tunnel he had just emerged from. Gradually it was getting closer; it sounded more like a high pitched scraping sound, similar to nails being dragged across a chalkboard. The feeling of dread returned to the pit of Max's stomach. He found himself looking into the tunnel, even though every fibre of his being was dreading what he may discover. The moment he glanced into the tunnel, he saw one of the plant monster's grotesque needle covered vines scraping its way towards him.

Instinctively he leapt back towards the foam obstacles. To his horror, he discovered that the vines were ripping through them from the other side. Turning back towards the side of the boat, he froze in terror. There it was again, the monster's enormous insidious bulbous head, constructed of deep self hatred and loathing. It was larger than before, so big that it dominated the area of the room. Its giant jagged interlocked needle teeth began to prize open, emitting a putrid smell, followed by a loud ringing sound which echoed throughout the room. As its colossal, carnivorous mouth widened, the gargantuan monster appeared to be inviting Max to willingly volunteer himself for a gruesome and grizzly death.

Max dived over the other side of the boat and onto the bouncy castle, closing his eyes in mid air. To his shock, when he landed, he was on his back on a patch of grass.

He was no longer in the Jolly Roger's Play Boat and the monster was nowhere to be seen. Sitting up Max turned his head and discovered he was next to a gravestone with his father's name on it.

He awoke with tears in his eyes. It took a few moments for him to compose himself. He lay on the bed, facing the sun kissed wall. Once again back in the present moment of reality, letting the numbness of sorrow wash over him. Even though it was painful to fully accept his father's death, it felt cathartic to witness himself feeling it. He no longer had the burden of avoiding or ignoring his feelings. Instead, he felt empowered by his lack of control. It felt as though he was floating on a wave that he had been trying so hard to push back, for so many years.

While his emotions washed over him, he recognised Fred's voice speaking to him from outside the door.

"Max, are you awake?" he softly inquired. Max cleared his throat and answered him.

Fred exclaimed with joy

"Ah brilliant! I've got my friend Raymond on the phone. Are you feeling up to meeting him this evening?"

Following his bout of emotions, Max felt a sense of euphoria and subsequently felt more positively about meeting Raymond.

"Outstanding, I'll go and tell him. And I'll make you a drink! It's almost time for your next pain killer." Fred announced on his way back to the telephone.

Max rolled over in the bed, exhaling from his injuries "Ah sh… it is time for some pain killers" he exclaimed. Breathing heavily he realised that the loud echoing ringing sound from his dream was more than likely Fred's 1970's landline telephone. But more alarmingly, he recognised that the putrid smell it belched out was actually his own breath.

Shortly afterwards, Max staggered out of the bedroom and sat in the living room with Fred, receiving his much needed pain medication.

Meanwhile Raymond was driving over to the flat. To his annoyance there was a number of road works in progress. Caught in a painfully tedious traffic jam, a mere stone's throw from Penelope Park, he drummed his fingers and thumbs upon his steering wheel. What was usually a 10 minute drive was quickly becoming a 20 minute waiting game. He began to gaze over at the park, recollecting how he first met Fred and what life would be like if he hadn't met him.

*HONK

"Move then!"

The disgruntled driver behind him shouted after rolling down his window. Following the alert, Raymond was pleasantly surprised to see that the traffic flow in front of him had started to progress. The make shift traffic light beside the cordoned off area stayed green just long enough for Raymond to pass. Much to the annoyance of the driver behind him, the lights immediately switched to red.

It wasn't long before he completed his journey, parking his car across the street from Fred's. While exiting and locking his vehicle, he heard the sound of a revving car engine.

"Wanker!" the driver from behind yelled out of his window as he sped past.

Raymond turned around to witness the car recklessly grind to a halt, bumping into the back of another car. Sighing in exhaustion, Raymond made his way towards Cabot's Court and got buzzed in. Taking the stairs he reached the outside balcony on the first floor. Before approaching the door, he took a moment to observe the tranquil greenery of Penelope Park.

When he was in his adolescence, the park was gaining a reputation for being a rough area. Groups of youths from rival schools would meet there and it soon became a breeding ground for violence. From what he had heard the park had been taken over by gangs. Yet, when he looked at it in the current moment, it had seemed to have transformed into a peaceful environment. People were going about their day in a relaxed manner without fear of threat.

Raymond felt a calming reassurance wash over him. He had a habit of being able to wait out negative feelings and finding a positive emotion to capture and hold on to. It was a skill that he had learned from Fred, one that he had been practicing so long that it now became like second nature to his subconscious.

Raymond had a key, but he decided to knock the door to give warning of his arrival. Fred promptly came to the door and greeted him in an excitable tone. A mere thirty feet away, Max was sat on the sofa trying to cover up the bloodstains on the cushion from the previous day. When Raymond finally entered the room, Max froze. He had been in countless primal situations over the past year. But somehow, the prospect of meeting a successful professional, which could have been him in another life, felt more intimidating than any of the desperate souls he had grown accustomed to living with. He stared at Raymond as if he was some unearthly being. Raymond quickly became aware of the social pressures that the haunted young man before him was presenting. He confidently, but respectfully, extended his hand and introduced himself. Upon their first contact, Max instantly felt more at ease in Raymond's presence.

He could see a great deal of Fred's influence within him. Following a brief interlude of ice breaking jokes and mandatory small talk; he felt a strong desire to discuss his latest interaction with the monster in his nightmare and the breakthrough about his father's death. However, it soon became apparent that there was a practical agenda in place. Max soon learned that Fred was concerned about his own health. Although it wasn't life threatening, he feared that he would not be able to offer his former student the support he needed, on his own. He planned to finance his rehabilitation at The Hope Centre, a private residential facility located on the outskirts of Carningsdale village.

Max jokingly asked

"Carningsdale? Isn't that where the criminally insane are held?"

"Ha, well, yes it is, but this facility is several miles away from there. The Hope Centre is widely regarded as one of the best rehabilitation centres in the country."

Fred replied, reassured to see that his troubled young friend had retained his sense of humour.

At first Max felt a glow of joy emitting from his chest. However, the feeling was short lived, as the weight of financial guilt sunk in.

Raymond, who had taken a seat on the adjacent sofa, quickly noticed Max's demeanour change. Although he remained silent he was observing the young man before him, fully aware of how important his support was to his survival. He started to see the weight of guilt flicker in the young man's eyes.

"It sounds expensive though."

Following his comment, Fred jovially responded, "The cost of not doing it would be substantially more. Besides, I heard that the Americans value a human life at around $9 million, so we're getting a bargain."

Sighing deeply, Max hesitated

"I'm not sure I deserve any of this. This is my mess, I've done all of this and I need to be the one to undo it. I should be helping other people. I mean, the stuff I've done to put that shit in my body is unbelievable."

As he continued, he felt emotions of sorrow pour out of him once more,

"People used to come to me for help."

Empathising with Max's conflict, Raymond gently interjected,

"It's a lot easier helping other people with their problems. There's a security in being able to be there for someone else. I used to liken it to a T.V. game show. See… the person being there for someone is like the audience, watching from the comfort of our own home, or under the dimmed lights of the studio. The person with the problem, they are the ones in the hot seat, under the pressure of emotions. The answers can seem simpler from where we are sitting and sometimes we want to scream it at them. But, we aren't the ones that have to feel vulnerable under the bright lights of observation. Now, I get the impression that you are in the middle of the show and it must be incredibly difficult."

Digesting Raymond's metaphor, Max nodded in agreement. He started to reflect on the times when he would listen to his friend's problems.

The group of friends he used to hang out with used to congregate around Penelope Park, before the park was cleaned up.

Each of them had experienced hardships and traumas. Max first met Misty at a house party, through a mutual friend. He first noticed her outside the window in the garden. Her short white furry jacket attracted his attention in the dimly lit garden. Leaning with her back against the wall, she was swigging an alcopop bottle; her unkempt brown hair partially covered her face.

She kept looking down the garden and away from the party. Sensing she was upset, Max went to talk to her. At first she tried to get him to go away, however, he quickly charmed his way past her defences with his sensitive nature.

He invited her to talk through her problems at a patio table at the bottom of the garden. It was darker at the table, but once they sat down, he could just about make out her face with the distant glow of the lighting from the house. It was clear she had been crying; her mascara had run down her freckled face. He soon learnt that her partner had cheated on her and had sadistically sent her pictures of the affair.

Misty Crisp had grown up in a broken home and was staying in a youth hostel in the North side of the city. She hated it there and would escape to Penelope Park whenever she could. She felt at ease talking to Max, although she had only just met him, he seemed to have a genuinely caring way about him. In some ways it came across as naivety, but it was a quality she hadn't seen much of in her fellow residents of Sanctuary House.

Max was implementing the counselling skills he had learnt from the course, but also naturally empathising with Misty. After an hour and a half of being heard and understood, Misty started to feel slightly better. The wounds were still very fresh from the malicious betrayal. However, he was slowly convincing her that not all guys were the scum of the earth.

While they continued to chat, Max started to hear an unusual noise. It was someone climbing over the wooden garden fence. Once the climber landed, Misty's face lit up as she sprang from her chair "Bingo!" she exclaimed, leaping towards the fence hopper and embracing them. "You alright love, how are you darling? I got your stuff." A male voice replied, before handing her something. While she walked back to the table, the figure scaled the fence and made a quick exit.

As Max began to ask who "Bingo" was, Misty ignited a rolled up cigarette. Within a few seconds the area started to stink of marijuana.

Misty took a toke of her joint before answering, "Bingo's my mate and he knows just how to make me feel good." She leaned towards Max and added "Can make you feel good too." Taking another drag she pulled him in for a kiss, exhaling the smoke into his mouth.

Max took a coughing fit and his sight started to go hazy. Misty giggled at Max as he spent a few moments trying to get his bearings and get used to the new sensation. "Better?" she asked.

"Mm." Max answered, somewhat hesitantly.

"Want some more?" she asked snickering and pouting

her lips.

He started to feel his anxieties take over, yet something within was telling him to continue with the experience. Before he knew what he was saying, he quickly exclaimed "I'm not even straight!"

Misty stared blankly at Max for a couple of seconds before bursting out into laughter. Still feeling confused and anxious, he started to crack up with laughter too.

Once Misty caught her breath she replied

"No wonder you're not a dickhead."

Through the course of their evening together, the two new friends exchanged phone numbers. Over the following weeks, Misty called upon Max when she felt low. It wasn't long before he met her friends; Zack Philips, Ben "Bingo" Ringo and Shaz Steele.

After they vacated Penelope Park, the five of them started to hang out around each other's houses, where they would lay about together chatting and experimenting with different drugs. At first Max got to know them each as individuals, listening to their problems and showing them compassion.

However, as his counselling course progressed, he was hearing other people's pain and struggles, both from his colleagues on the course and from his friends on the outside.

It was a never ending cycle of pain and discomfort. Although it felt as though he had been reliving his montage of memories for an hour, it had only been a few minutes. Raymond could tell Max's mind had travelled to another time zone. He tactfully commented,

"It sounds like you care a great deal for other people and how you can help them."

Max instantaneously replied,

"I should have been stronger for them; they didn't have the advantages I had. I don't even know where they are anymore! I don't deserve any help until I can make things right for them!"

his voice became increasingly flustered with each sentence. Compassionately raising his hand Raymond calmly interjected,

"It's okay Max; I can hear there's a great deal of pain in your voice. You feel responsible for other people's pain."

Max's body started to shake and his face reddened with emotion,

"I am responsible; I was the only one in a position to put things right for them. I thought I could become a better counsellor and gain a better understanding by experiencing the drugs with them. It's no bloody wonder my Dad left!"

A pregnant pause befell the room. Raymond could see the wheels in Max's head began to turn, his eyes drifted from towards the floor while he processed the weight and power of his closing statement.

"That's a powerful statement. I'm wondering how it feels to hear yourself say that?"

After a thought filled pause, still staring deeply into the ground, Max answered,

"It feels like the truth."

Raymond glanced over at Fred. He was sat at his dining table, his tear soaked eyes fixated on Max. Looking back to the broken young man before him, he asked,

"When did you last see your father?"

Sniffling and clearing his throat Max replied,

"It was before my 8th Birthday. He was supposed to turn up for that. It doesn't matter so much now though; the twat died just after I started the counselling course. That was around the time I met my friends with the drugs in Penny Park."

Raymond commented

"You haven't seen him since you were 7 and he died just before you started taking recreational drugs? I think it matters more than you may think."

Max defensively sighed

"He was an arsehole for leaving but, if I hadn't acted up the way I did he might not have. My primary school headmaster all but confirmed it. I should have thanked him for leaving to be honest; since he left I saw things differently. I paid more attention to people; it helped me to develop empathy."

Raymond took a moment to contain his anger at the thought of a headmaster imprinting such a horrible thought on to a child's mind. He arose from the sofa and approached the dining table where Fred was sat. Exchanging an understanding glance with his mentor he retrieved an empty chair and brought it over to the sofa area.

"Okay Max, if it's alright with you I'd like to do an experiment?"

Max silently agreed, nodding his head. Raymond smiled and gestured to the empty chair.

"I want you to imagine there's a seven year old boy in that chair. Imagine his father has just left him. What would you say to him?"

To his surprise, Max felt a boiling rage emerge from his stomach up into his chest. His voice trembled with anger as he addressed the imaginary child,

"Your head teacher was wrong!"

Raymond encouraged,

"Good. Yes he was. Is that seven year old responsible for your father leaving?"

"No!"

he replied, his voice shaking and raw with emotion from the pit of his stomach.

Visceral tears poured down his face as he let the realisation sink in.

Fred poured a glass of water and brought it over to Max, sitting next to him and placing his hand on his shoulder supportively.

"See Max, we can often feel self blame for things that aren't our fault. Now your friends from Penelope Park who took the drugs, they would have each had their reasons for taking them. But you were not personally responsible for any of them. It was their choices much like it was yours. Experimenting with drugs will not enhance your career as a counsellor. But, acknowledging and exploring the deep rooted pain that can lead to taking them… that will."

Once Max composed himself, he reinitiated eye contact with Raymond and explained

"I know I'm not responsible for them, but I still feel it. It still feels wrong to financially burden Fred with the fees of the Hope Centre too."

Raymond reassured him

"You're a human being and you're caring about other human beings… its human nature. Now, if it was 10 – 15 years ago, I'm fairly certain Fred wouldn't have asked me for help. He would have considered it his burden to carry. But, now he's not as young as he used to be, he wanted me to be around to support you. I can see that you're struggling with accepting the guilt and shame associated with your addiction and the damage it's caused to others. But, you know that your chances of success are more likely with professional support. If it helps, think of other people you want to help in your position. You look like you've been through a war and make no mistake, you are still in one. Getting through this addiction with altered brain chemicals and demons, that could cause you to go back, will be a fight; potentially every day."

Following Raymond's comments, Fred cleared his throat and softly enquired,

"I have to ask, did you even see your counsellor throughout all of this?"

Max slowly shook his head,

"I saw her once and got the paperwork filled out. Shaz forged her signature for the first eight sessions on the paperwork. By that point I was off the course."

All of a sudden, Max began to feel faint and weary. He was feeling the seismic internal shift in his emotions, after delving into his memories and confronting the guilt at the epicentre of his self loathing. He sipped his water and thanked them for their support, accepting Fred's offer. A mutual feeling of relief and joy fell upon the room. The feeling immediately boosted Max's energy levels.

It felt surreal how many emotions he had experienced in such a short period of time. As the evening progressed the conversations shifted to less intense topics. He learnt about Raymond's experiences in Penelope Park and how he may have gone down a different path in life if he hadn't met Fred when he did. The story enabled Max to take his mind off his own past. Hearing how Raymond had battled through adversity to become a highly skilled counsellor also inspired him. As the sun began to set and the evening darkened, hunger started to strike. Raymond clasped his hands together

"Max, mate, how do you feel about a Chinese?"

Max's face lit up, he had almost forgotten about the concept of takeaway food. Fred promptly retrieved a menu and readied the phone. He and Raymond had shared many a takeaway meal over the years; however, they mutually had a soft spot for Chinese takeaway. It had become somewhat of a tradition on special occasions. Within the hour, they each had a freshly prepared meal courtesy of the Double Dragon. The scent of Chow Mein entered the room. Prizing the plastic container open, Max savoured the moment as the warm steam brushed his face and the smell of sweet and sour sauce entered his nose. While they consumed their meals, Max started to talk about his time at South Town Harbour. Both Raymond and Fred found it difficult to believe how the seemingly abandoned area could have been hiding so many tortured souls.

"I know it sounds ridiculous. But then again, in a city where an Anglo Saxon Re-enactment group were responsible for clearing out Penelope Park, it isn't that farfetched."

Fred remarked,

"Well I suppose the people who used to loiter in the park

must have gone somewhere. We should probably notify the police. Whatever's going on down there, there's quite a lot of risk to people's lives."

Raymond took a break from eating

"Well, how do you feel about that Max?"

Suddenly, Max was hit with a vivid flashback to his rape. His stomach churned and his throat tightened. His body started to reject the succulent meal he was enjoying just a few seconds previously. Dropping his fork, he darted towards the toilet. Reaching his target in milliseconds, Max projectile vomited into the toilet.

Raymond and Fred looked at each other in shock at the sudden and violent reaction. While Max occupied the toilet, Raymond quietly stated

"There's a lot of trauma to work through here."

Fred's gaze subtly lowered to the blood stain on the sofa,

"Undoubtedly. I don't think he should be going anywhere near that harbour. That being said, it sounds like a number of people's lives may be at risk."

Finishing the last of his meal, Raymond mumbled

"Mm, once we get him set up at the Hope Centre, I'll look into it."

By the following night, Fred had somewhat miraculously secured Max's place at the Hope Centre, for 6 months intensive rehabilitation.

The intense conversations exploring the recovering addict's troubled past, gave him insights into himself, building a foundation of self acceptance; a crucial aspect to his recovery.

Raymond drove Fred and Max up to the Hope Centre the following day. When he got into the car, it became painfully evident that his body and mind were still only just beginning to heal from the abuse it had taken. The seat provided him with support and as much comfort as possible. But, when Raymond inadvertently made a turn, slightly too sharply, Max exhaled sharply as he became very aware of the tenderness of his backside.

After apologising Raymond ensured the rest of the journey was smooth and slow. The radio was playing but Max was in a world of his own, gazing out of the window, observing the urban terrain of the "Sea-Side City".

He started to feel anxious; concerned that one of Candy-Shilling's underlings may see him. While he was reflecting and recuperating in the comfort of Fred's flat, Max's mind was focused on exploring his past.

Now he was back in a car, he kept looking out for the hooded figures that he saw stalking him before. While they were slowly edging through early morning traffic jams, in the more built up areas of the city, it felt as though he was trapped in a gold fish bowl. But to his relief, he couldn't see anyone.

Once they made it out of the city and the pace of the journey quickened, things began to feel better. Max was almost in a hypnotic state, staring at the green blur of the bushes and fields. Finally, they turned into an inclining side road leading to a small car park. Even though the world had turned several times in Max's head during his trance, the journey was complete within an hour.

Coming to, Max observed his new home for the next few months. The Hope Centre was a large, two floor building. Raymond and Fred escorted him up a pebbled path into the entrance.

Once they entered a lady behind the counter booked Max in. Following a brief tour of the premises, Raymond and Fred joined Max for a tea before they left. They reassured him that they would be in touch…

CHAPTER 7:
THE HOPE CENTRE

Over the following weeks Max gradually underwent a metamorphosis. With the appropriate care and support, the physical withdrawal symptoms he had experienced so intensely, slowly started to lose their power over him. Each week a different aspect of his freedom became restored. He went through a consistent structured routine of exercise, diet and counselling. As he looked in the mirror each morning, his physical appearance slowly re-emerged. Fred would phone every week and Raymond would drive him up to visit in person on the weekends. After a couple of weeks Max joined one of the therapy groups that the Hope Centre provided.

The facility also offered a variety of different therapy groups, each designed to encourage clients to discuss their addictions and support one another through their respective journeys. Group members consisted of both residential clients and part time clients, often further along in their rehabilitation. The part time clients would check in with the group to continue their personal progress and support the full time members.

The sessions were held by a facilitator specially trained in holding the emotions of the group. Max was apprehensive at first. However, he forced himself to attend to continue his progression towards recovery. During the earlier sessions he refrained from speaking, he simply sat there and listened to his peer's experiences. There was no pressure for members to talk, but the more he attended, the more he felt encouraged to open up. He found the other members to be incredibly honest in their disclosures. As the weeks progressed and his growth and trust within the environment developed, he became inspired to open up in the third week. By the forth week he found himself disclosing some of his most personal and intimate aspects of his life.

Through his personal counselling he had come to terms with the impact his parents' divorce had taken on his self esteem. Unusually, during the session that week, there was a new member who had joined the group. The new arrival was one of his friends from Penelope Park, Zack Philips.

At the start of the session they briefly greeted each other. Max was anxious to know about the safety of their other friends, following the months he hadn't seen them. But to his surprise, Zack seemed reserved and dismissive. In addition to his dismissive attitude he had completely changed his style of clothing. Previously he was contented to wear baggy t-shirts and cargo trousers, both covered in cigarette burn holes. Now he was wearing an expensive looking leather jacket, designer clothing and tinted glasses. But in spite of his expensive appearance, he also seemed to be void of any emotion.

Max suspected that he was wearing them as defensive armour, in fear of the new setting he had joined. The feelings resonated with Max due to how he felt the first week he had joined the group. In an effort to both challenge himself and encourage the new member to do the same, he decided to bring his feelings towards his estranged parents to the group. He had identified them as a key trigger in his addiction. To his relief the group held him with support and understanding. He felt accepted and in turn was able to accept himself.

After the fifth week, Max's body was almost entirely back to normal physically and he had never felt better mentally. At this point in his journey, he was ready to delve deeper into the roots of what had caused his pain. His therapist was a young woman named Silver. Although she had only been counselling professionally for two years, she had a calming way about her. Despite not having the experience of Fred or Raymond, there was a refreshing uniqueness to the space she provided.

Although there was a structured programme in place, he was also empowered to explore his thoughts.

During these moments, Max often visualised himself as an artist in front of a blank canvas, with the ability to explore and express his pain without fear of judgement.

He entered the cream coloured counselling room and took his seat on the light brown leather reclining chair facing the window. Silver pushed her long, straightened blonde hair to the side of her face and welcomed him with a warm smile. Max wanted to pick up where they left off the previous week. During their previous session, he recalled his nightmares with the giant plant at The Jolly Roger's Play Boat, which had lead their focus towards his relationship with his absent father.

They quickly identified that the headmaster's verbal assault and his father being absent from his 8th Birthday; were critical weaknesses in the foundation of his self esteem, causing him to subconsciously blame himself for his father's neglect. But after the session she had invited him to consider how this may have impacted his life.

Throughout the week, Max had started to think about his sexuality. Previously he believed he had always accepted it. But the more he thought about it, the more he recalled often feeling shame whenever he would think of acting upon his desires, or even admitting his sexuality in public. Following his reflections, he quickly began the session explaining how he felt.

"It was like this stomach churning feeling of dread and guilt. At first it was almost instantly, I sort of associated it with the stigma of being gay. I'd tell someone for the first time or I'd see a guy I liked the look of and within a few minutes I'd start to feel anxious. Over time and the more I associated with people who accepted me, the feelings wouldn't hit me as quickly. I just assumed they went away. But looking back, I'd feel the same feelings, but it would just take longer for them to surface."

Sliver's eyes glistened with understanding,

"You're reliving the guilt of your father leaving every time you feel something for another human being?"

Max nodded, taking a moment to hear what he knew to be true. Although he had come to the conclusion himself, hearing it aloud for the first time enabled him to gain a deeper understanding of his experiences.

She added

"That's a heavy burden for anyone to carry, especially a developing young mind."

"It was more manageable before, when I could just avoid it. As a teenager I'd just focus on other things like my school work or helping others. It wasn't until I joined the University counselling course the other year, when I found it was more difficult. It felt increasingly difficult to contain my feelings and everyone else in the course had been through so much more. I felt angry at myself; I just wanted to be able to focus on helping others more effectively. My friends were into drugs and I used to tell myself I was taking them as research. But now I see that the more I took them, the more I needed them to buy me more time away from the feelings of dread."

Silver replied,

"I hear you saying it was more manageable, but avoiding and containing your feelings sounds like quite a difficult way of living."

Max felt warmth within his chest. He started to recognise how the underlying resentment he had held for himself had crippled his self esteem. Instantly a weight had been lifted from his soul, he visualised discovering and removing a slimy, tar-like, parasite that had been undetectably feeding off him for years.

Following his cathartic self discovery, the remainder of the session passed quite quickly. After leaving the room, he walked with a renewed sense of purpose and acceptance. However, his resolve would soon be tested during the group. Following the previous week's meeting and his recent one to one session, Max was looking forward to reconnecting with the group and continuing his progress. However, his resolve would soon be tested during the group session.

He had attempted to reconnect with Zack during the week but he was unable to find him. As the session began, he realised there was a substitute group mediator. Although the members of the group were sat in chairs in a circle as usual, the change in leadership dramatically changed how the session was led. A few minutes after the session started, Zack strutted in. He was still wearing his leather jacket and tinted glasses. Although it had been over a year since Max had been in his company, something felt different about Zack. While spending time with Misty and Bingo he would sit with his back against the wall and play his guitar. Other than the music he played, he didn't say much, but he always seemed content to be around his friends. The Zack Max saw in the group seemed guarded, bitter and almost hostile.

As he slumped in his seat and tried to get comfortable, Zack sighed in frustration,

"Alright, I'll start. My name's Zack and I'm an addict. Truthfully, my manager sent me here because I'm a bloody good guitarist and he wants me back on tour, mainly because… the band is a bit crap without me."

Some of the other members of the group appeared to be irritated by his attitude and others questioned what authority his manager had over him and whether he felt that his only worth was his musical talents. When challenged by the other group members, Zack sank back into his chair, clearly frustrated at the experience.

The mediator of the group controlled the situation and addressed the defence mechanisms. She encouraged the group not to challenge Zack too much, as it was only his second week in attendance and he may not be ready to explore challenges yet. Once the tension had settled, the group continued to express their experiences, each checking in with how they felt.

A woman in her thirties, named Sarah, disclosed how she was close to relapsing because a male colleague at work had been making unwanted sexual advances to her. Her disclosure instantly reminded Max of his unconscious rape at South Town Harbour.

While the rest of the group were focused on Sarah's disclosure, Zack was feeling resentful and bitter at the other member's reaction to his arrogant introduction. Unbeknown to the mediator, or the other members, behind the cool rims of his spectacles his heated head was seething. All of a sudden, he interrupted,

"Oh come on that's bollocks, you probably wanted him and got pissed off when you found out he was joking."

Before the rest of the group could react, Max turned to Zack and sharply questioned

"What the hell is wrong with you? Have you any idea how damaging sexual assaults are?"

Zack chirped back,

"I'm a Rock Star mate, there's nothing wrong with me. While you and the rest of them lot went down to that scummy little harbour, my uncle got me signed to 'Time Tomb'."

Max felt himself burn up with anger,

"Well while you were being a 'Rock Star' for a year, my body was being used against my will while I was unconscious!"

Despite the harrowing declaration from his former friend, Zack aggressively and defensively responded,

"You're a junkie and you're gay! Drug addicts make love to get their fix all the time!"

Max felt a fire flicker within him, the tensions escalated by the second. Scarlet red and filled with fury, he arose from his chair. In that instant he wanted to murder Zack, time froze. His body pumped with adrenaline, Max's eyes darted to meet Zack's. He saw fear start to sink into Zack, whose cool demeanour began to crack. The rest of the group were silently observing, stricken with fear and anxiety, as if they were watching a car crash. Sensing the situation had reached a boiling point he looked to the mediator. She too appeared to be overcome with fear, despite her role as mediator.

Breathing quickly with anger, Max managed to control his rage and began to walk out of the room. Before he left he responded,

"Whatever it was that happened to me... it wasn't love."

With that he left the room, the tears welling up in his eyes. A millisecond after Max had left, the woman who Zack had originally interrupted sprung from her seat. She lunged at Zack and punched him in the face, shattering his glasses and knocking him out of his chair. Max could hear the commotion taking place in the group; as he walked down the smooth and shiny cream coloured corridor.

He intended to go to his room, however, before he could fully process what had occurred he found Raymond waiting for him by the rock fountain in the reception area.

"Max! Are you ok mate?"

Raymond asked with concern.

"I'm fine, just been a hard day."

Max replied, swallowing the frog in his throat and wiping

away his tears. Raymond approached him,

"Shall we grab a drink and take it to your room?"

he asked in a soft voice. Max nodded and they made their way back to his accommodation via the tea vender. During Raymond and Fred's visits they would usually go back to his room, however, this was the first time that Raymond had asked to go there. Max instantly detected that something had changed. He thought that they may be discussing the prospect of moving on and life outside of the Hope Centre. Progressing down the sunlit concrete corridor, Max was starting to feel better, becoming more distanced from the heated incident within the group.

When they reached his room, Max opened his beech fire proof door and led his guest in. Once they entered, it became apparent from Raymond's demeanour that something was weighing heavily on his mind. He paced nervously, loosening his tie from his collar. Looking around the room, nervous of making eye contact with his recovering friend, he noticed the mirror at Max's dressing table.

He caught a glance of himself and swiftly pulled out the chair, facing it towards the bed. Raymond had always presented a cool and calming aura. Sensing his discomfort, Max felt feelings of anxiety the more he saw him.

"Max, can we sit down?"

"What's wrong?"

he replied, his voice quaking. Raymond gestured for him to sit on the bed while taking a sip of his tea. The young man started to reply with panic in his voice. Raymond interrupted sternly

"Fred's passed away..."

Time stopped, Max's head and face went numb as the information entered his ears. Within a millisecond his legs lowered him to a seated position on his bed.

"But I just talked to him last week... How..."

"I'm sorry Max, its hit me like a ton of bricks too. I'm not sure how he died, it's still being investigated. I realise this is a hell of a shock."

Max nodded, silently trying to comprehend the loss of such a crucial part of his life.

"When did this happen?"

he finally asked in confusion, still not fully able to accept that he was really dead.

"It was four days ago. I've been making a lot of phone calls and attending to a lot of his affairs as I'm the executer of his will. But, I thought it was important to come and see you face to face with this."

As the two friends continued to chat and commemorate the loss of their late friend, the subject of the funeral was broached. It was a difficult topic, the thought of attending such a difficult event made Max feel incredibly intimidated and vulnerable. He found himself in a vice like dilemma.

"If I don't go, I'm going to regret it for the rest of my days. But, I'm worried that if I do, it will be too much. Both of these situations could cause me to relapse." Max explained, his voice quaking with uncertainty and pressure. Raymond calmly sipped his tea and replied,

"In all honesty Max, you're absolutely right. People have relapsed because of situations like this. But, life will throw you… any number of situations, which may cause you to relapse. You won't have to face them alone, but you are strong enough to face them. That being said, I think we both know that Fred wouldn't want you to feel pressured to come, or not to come. It's a choice for you and one which he and I would and will support."

Max pondered Raymond's words of honesty and compassion. It occurred to him that he had not yet been back to Rockshore since his admission to the Hope Centre. Before he could make his decision, he thought it would be prudent to assess how he felt returning to the "Sea-Side City". Articulating his process to his friend, Raymond agreed to take a field trip back to the city the following morning. Following their discussion, Max guided him back to the reception entrance point.

Once Raymond had left, Max felt alone again. The calming rock fountain and warm atmosphere of the area, started to feel cold and almost superficial. He walked back down the corridor to his room in a numbed state. The light concrete corridor was empty, but his head was filled with confusion and sorrow; trapped between thoughts of his rape and Fred's death.

A deep sinking feeling grew from his chest to his stomach. With all of the progress Max had achieved during the weeks of positive rebuilding, he hadn't experienced such an intense onslaught of negative emotions for some time.

When he got to his door, he found the group mediator waiting for him.

"Hello, I just wanted to check in with you and see how you were feeling, after everything that happened in the group this afternoon. Usually I try and stay out of the group as much as possible, but I should have stepped in more today."

When faced with a virtual stranger showing concern, Max quickly masked the situation,

"I'm alright; I try to look at these things as challenges. I'd be lying if I said I wasn't disappointed about how Zack has changed but…"

She quickly interrupted,

"Zack has been removed from the Hope Centre and so is Sarah, the young lady who assaulted him."

After pausing, she added

"I realise I'm somewhat of an outsider here. But if you do feel effected at any point please find someone to talk to, we have people available on call at all times."

Max nodded, concerned that she saw through his false positivity. Before opening the door, he agreed he would seek out a counsellor if he needed to in the evening. As Max entered his room, it became increasingly more apparent that he was trapped alone with his thoughts. He felt incredibly low.

The feeling intensified as thoughts of relapse crept into his mind. Although his mind was repulsed by the idea, his body began to crave it. Unable to sit with himself he hurriedly left the room to go to the onsite cafeteria. As luck would have it, when he arrived the cafeteria was almost empty.

Max ordered a large roast dinner and a custard pudding. He knew he was eating as a coping mechanism, but this time he was aware of it and it was by choice. Although he recognised it wasn't healthy, he was making a conscious decision to avoid a disastrous alternative. Mentally, each mouthful was an attempt to fill an un-fillable void. But due to the healthy balanced diet he had become accustomed to, the onslaught of food was taking its toll on his body.

When he finally got round to his custard pudding, he recalled the fateful incident his eight year old self endured in school, which had contributed to such destruction. If young Toby Kenny hadn't spat in his custard, he wouldn't have gone to the headmasters office and been burdened with the guilt and self blame of his parent's divorce and his father's neglect. Looking at the custard he started to snicker to himself. Picking up the plastic spoon he started to eat the custard. With the speed he had consumed his main meal the custard was still warm. As the first spoonful entered his mouth and his taste buds registered the flavour, it was the sweetest thing he had ever tasted. It was as if the custard had been seasoned with psychological redemption. His pace of consumption slowed, allowing him to enjoy every mouthful.

Once he was finished, he began to feel extremely bloated but contentedly fed thanks to his magical custard experience.

Max had successfully numbed his haunted mind with food. Staggering back to his room once again, he drifted past several others who were making their way to the cafeteria.

The vast array of mental activity mixed with the culinary

coping behaviours had rendered him into a relaxed and docile state. When he finally made it back to his room, he drank a glass of water and perched on his bed, looking out of his window at the tree branches swaying in the wind. After a few moments his eyes began to get heavy, causing his body to slowly retreat to laying down on the bed. Before he knew it he had drifted into a deep food coma.

Several hours later he awoke. It was night time and the moonlight shone through the now darkened bushes outside. Gingerly and slowly Max arose from his bed, yawning and stretching his torso. He climbed into bed with the intention of going back to sleep. Unfortunately, it wasn't long before he was reminded of Zack's comments about his sexual assault. Eventually he gave up trying to sleep and exited the bed once more. He decided to keep his promise and go and seek out someone to talk to. Putting on a hoody on top of the clothing he fell asleep in, he set off to leave the room.

Suddenly, something caught his eye across the moon lit floor.

The shadows of the bushes appeared to be consuming the light. A sickeningly familiar feeling of dread emitted from his stomach. He edged towards the door in an effort to leave the room, but he froze in fear. He was unable to move any further and he was too terrified to turn around and face what he knew was behind him. His eyes locked down on the moon lit floor, the shadowy vines beckoned him to turn around.   Both petrified and defiant he remained frozen. Despite his best efforts to ignore it, the monster had returned.

A darkened and rotting vine slithered past him and wrapped itself around the door handle to his room. In his state of terror, Max noticed that the vine no longer had needles attached to it. The floor darkened further as the silhouette of its bulbous pod head engulfed the light. With each movement, the sound of rustling leaves could be heard etching closer to him. Max jolted forward in intimidation.

To his horror, a husky demonic voice hissed

"So... you've killed another father figure..."

Shocked, Max's eyes widened and his gaze rose to see a mirror on the door, revealing his terrifying tormentor's new form. Its head now resembled a rotting plant; its needle like teeth had been reduced to decaying fly trap spines. It's head tilted, moving closer as it continued to venomously taunt

"Soon you won't have anyone left. How many other lives will you drain with your attention seeking ways?"

The plant may have lost its needles, but its words pierced his soul deeper than the threat of physical harm. Sensing the pain it was inflicting, the plant whispered

"Where are you going... back to the Shag-Pile? You certainly got enough attention there."

The evil plant chuckled, revelling in its victim's anguish.

"We can end this here and now... there's no need to leave."

After enduring the monster's wounding words; Max felt a fury that allowed him to regain his ability to move. Walking purposefully towards the doorway he gripped the vine covered handle. To his surprise, the vine felt weak and withering, similar to a strand of cobweb. As he twisted the handle, the plant monster let out a howling roar. Still gripping the door handle Max turned to face his towering floral tormentor.

Though it still consumed the room in size and it filled him with dread, he finally saw it for what it truly was. No longer able to hide behind the weaponised illusion of killer drugs, the plant was merely a parasite. Through his hard work, Max realised that it was merely the darker side of himself. It became clear that his abilities of empathy and compassion were darkly mirrored by the entity's scathing judgement and hatred. A monster created by self blame and guilt, lurking in a darkened corner of his mind, able to manifest itself anywhere he went and feed off of his fears and doubts.

But, the monster's power over him had weakened, much like it's appearance.

His subconscious had become aware that he was dreaming and that everything he had seen and heard was a fiction.

With a swift motion he opened the door, revealing the light from the corridor. He watched in satisfaction and relief as the shadowy plant monster's vines gradually evaporated, like smoke, in the glow of the light. He knew it may return, but he also knew that he had the power to take back control and leave it in the darkened crevice that it had spawned from. With that he left the room and subsequently he awoke with a start.

Instantly sitting up, he looked to the side of the room. To his relief he saw nothing but the shadows from bushes outside swaying. He also heard the wind howling through the window. He had escaped the jaws of the carnivorous plant once again.

Once he caught his breath from the jolt of his nightmare, he felt a feeling of accomplishment and swiftly drifted off back to sleep.

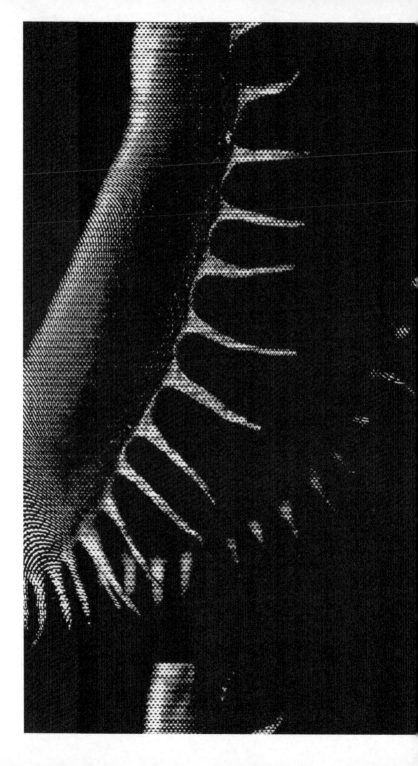

CHAPTER 8:
RETURN TO THE "SEA-SIDE CITY"

The following morning, he woke up earlier than usual and decided to use the gym facilities before breakfast. Raymond was picking him up at 10 AM and although he was looking forward to facing the challenge of returning to Rockshore, he wanted to maintain the discipline of his routine for his recovery.

At 9:50 Max was waiting in the reception area. He was dressed in a white t-shirt and a pair of jeans, which Fred had brought up for him during one of his earlier visits. Sitting on the bench, where Raymond was waiting for him the previous day, he reflected how far he had come since he had last visited Rockshore. Observing the flow of water cascading down the rock fountain, calmness fell over him. Not only had his physical injuries healed, he felt content with himself.

When he was squatting at the harbour, even before the addiction fully took control of him, he found himself in a constant state of resentment. But now, he was able to look back at himself with compassion and understanding, a quality he used to only reserve for others. It wasn't long before the familiar sight of Raymond's car caught his eye, as it pulled into the drive. Max got to his feet and promptly came out to join his friend. Raymond put his hand up to greet Max and reached over to open his car door. Once he got in the car they promptly set off for their journey,

"You seem in better spirits today, Max, you're looking well."

"I guess you caught me on an off day yesterday. I'm still saddened to hear about Fred though. I can't believe he's gone. I wish I could have thanked him." Max swallowed down trying to fight the tension in his throat.

"Well to be honest, you've thanked him in the most meaningful way you could have. He saw the changes within you over the past few weeks."

Raymond's comments reassured Max, allowing him to feel a sense of relief. While they continued to chat and half listen to the ambient music on the radio, Max took in the sights from the car window. The sun glistened through the trees, creating flickers of shade while they passed down the narrow country roads of Carningsdale. In a gentle contrast to the previous car journeys Max had experienced, he was no longer suffering from paranoia or physical injury. Subsequently, he could more confidently rely on the accuracy of his senses.

His ears instantly perked up when he overheard the radio DJ announce

"And here's the new hit single 'Bingo'n too far' from 'Time Tomb'."

Despite his newly found confidence in his senses, Max found himself in a state of disbelief as he turned up the radio. He recognised the guitar riff that followed within an instant. It was a song that Zack had jokingly composed about their friend and local dealer Ben "Bingo" Ringo, during the times they hung out.

"Oh, this band's got a local lad in it hasn't it? Do you know him?"

Raymond asked, noticing the volume had increased.

"I used to; funny thing is I was there when he wrote this."

Max started to chuckle as he remembered the origin of the song, before explaining,

"Bingo and Misty were friends with benefits for years, but over time Shaz and Bingo started to develop feelings for each other. One night we were all sat in Misty's room and she was cuddled up with Bingo. Shaz was fine with it at first, but eventually she snapped and shouted 'This has been going too far'. It was a really tense moment, until Zack sang 'Baby its Bingo'n too far' and proceeded to strum out the song we're listening to now."

Raymond giggled in amazement,

"That's incredible, I just read about him the other day. His uncle's a record producer and he got him connected with the other lot in London. They made it big with this song over in America, but he was causing some problems on tour so his manager pulled him."

Max sighed,

"Yeah, I saw him at the centre."

Turning to look at Max in surprise, Raymond enquired as to how their reunion went.

He didn't want to reveal what had happened within the group to uphold confidentiality. He knew he could trust Raymond, but he still didn't want to personally discuss what had happened within the group. Instead he simply answered,

"I don't think he's changed for the better. But I need to focus on my own fight at this stage."

Although they were both enjoying the journey, Raymond was aware that their trip back into the city was unfamiliar territory for Max. He had grown up in the Sea-Side City, but where his life had become controlled by desperation and despair, the memories of the city he once knew had mutated. In some ways it was as though he was going into a minefield. The risks of triggering emotions which may cause a relapse were infinite. With this in mind, Raymond commented

"Going back here today is a big step. It may not feel like it and I hope that it doesn't. But, if you want to go back to the Hope Centre at any point, just say the word. It's important to have safety strategies in place if you need them."

Max nodded, acknowledging the potential challenges ahead of him. In a humorous shift he jokingly commented

"I haven't had an ice cream in ages."

To his pleasant surprise, Raymond informed him that there was a new ice cream parlour which had opened up in the city centre. By this point they had made it into the city and Raymond headed for their new destination of the "Cone-ee-Island" ice cream parlour.

Their journey through the city was swift, but from what Max saw, the buildings seemed less depressing and grey than before. Each sight he took in seemed to look brighter, seasoned with positive potential.

Before he knew it, Raymond had swung his car into a parking space near the back of the Town Hall. Exiting the car, he started to feel uneasy. He couldn't remember what had happened several weeks prior, due to his concussion and the psychotic hallucinations he was suffering at the time. But, subconsciously, he sensed that they were within the vicinity where he had reunited with Fred.

Taking care not to become consumed by his feelings, Max took a couple of deep breaths and drew his focus to Raymond. They made their way down the street towards the Cone-ee-Island ice cream parlour. Max stopped to look at his surroundings, it became clear to him that there had been some sort of incident which had occurred in the area during his time in the Hope Centre. He noticed that several windows in the street had been smashed and boarded up.

"Did something happen down here?"

He asked Raymond.

"Sorry?"

Raymond replied, scanning the area, he quickly identified what Max was referring to,

"Ah yes, there was a bit of trouble down here just over a month ago. Some sort of bar fight broke out and escalated into a riot. The paper reckons it was started by some young racist that had a gripe with the Uni, pretty unbelievable how quickly this sort of thing can escalate. It looks a lot better than it did a few weeks back though."

As he continued down the street, the thought of the damage being reduced over time, gave Max a feeling of hope. It was as if he was surrounded by an analogy for his personal journey of change. He visualised the damage that would have been caused during the riot. The smashed windows, the debris in the street and the chaotic emotions of anger, fear and rebellion in those involved. But through time, the tensions had settled, the debris had been cleared and all that was left was the start of repairs.

While he continued to take in his surroundings, he noticed the people within the area appeared comfortable to be going about their lives in the present moment; indifferent to what had happened previously.

Navigating their way through a number of people heading towards the Town Square, he started to find the sea of faces overwhelming. It was a Saturday morning and the sounds of chatter echoed across the area. Despite the unfamiliarity of the busy environment, he was able to walk with his head held high.

Suddenly, his attentions were drawn to a couple of thuggish looking men who were swaggering towards him. They seemed familiar, yet he couldn't recollect where he had encountered them before. He couldn't help but sense danger from them.

The fragmented emotions and memories caused him to stare at them. One of them clocked him looking at them,

"What's this prick staring at?"

he asked as the other turned his attention to Max.

"I don't know! I've never seen him in my life."

Hearing them speak caused Max to avert his gaze from them. As they passed him grimacing, he remembered that they had threatened to beat him up in Jacksville while he was on his way back to South Town Harbour. The fact they didn't recognise him, reminded him of how much his appearance had changed since the start of his journey.

"Who were those two?" Raymond asked, looking back at them in concern.

Max explained the situation to him. Although he reassured him that his appearance had changed, Raymond also joked

"I doubt you'll be the only one they've threatened with violence and I doubt you'll be the only one they don't recognise afterwards."

Shortly after the encounter, they approached the parlour. It was an American style ice cream parlour, it's red border illuminated by the neon "Cone-ee-Island" sign. The shiny black and white chequered floor showcased the cleanliness of the wholesome family environment they were entering.

The parlour was moderately busy, as expected on a weekend. Several families and a table with three male students were sitting in the establishment, however, Raymond and Max didn't have to wait long for their ice creams.

A large friendly young man named Henry served them. Max had a small pot of plain vanilla ice cream and Raymond had a large caramel chocolate milkshake. There were tables available towards the back of the venue, near the young men. Max was in two minds whether to sit in or take their treats to go. While Henry prepared their treats and they contemplated their options, Max started to overhear the young men's conversation.

"Have either of you guys heard from Shelly lately?"

An athletic young man with dark brown hair asked in an

American accent. One of his friends shook his head, unable to talk with the chocolate Sunday he was consuming.

His other friend snidely interjected in a cockney accent,

"JJ mate, you got a whole city full of birds here. She's clearly banging that pasty nervous kid she brought down here. I still can't believe she took him to that old harbour, everyone knows it's crawling with tramps and druggies."

The young American snarled,

"You're such an asshole Terry! They obviously made it out fine; she was down here the next day. She knows what she was doing, she's a goddamn psychologist. Besides, that was weeks ago, she's probably on vacation again. What do you think Oz?"

The other young man quirkily replied

"I don't know, to be honest that was the last time we saw her. Maybe she's harbouring a grudge."

The other two instantly broke out into groans over their friend's harbour pun. Meanwhile at the counter, thoughts of the harbour were echoing in Max's mind once again. As soon as he had heard the talk about "that old harbour", he knew they were referring to South Town Harbour. The hairs on his neck had stood up and the memories of pain came flooding back. He found himself breathing heavier as his mind took him back to the dark place he once squatted, the physical injuries he had endured and the intense pain he couldn't quite remember. Raymond could tell something had changed in his demeanour,

"You alright?"

Max's distant gaze refocused back to Raymond,

"Yeah... yeah, I... think we should take our stuff to go if that's alright? There's something I need to talk to you about."

"Sure mate, yeah. We'll get going as soon as we get these."

"Cool." Max replied, silently managing his memories through subtle breathing exercises.

Once they were presented with their order, they swiftly left the parlour.

Upon opening the door, Max felt the fresh cool breeze hit his face; it was as if he had managed to serve a sentence in his own personal prison. Ironically, the ice cream parlour was surprisingly hot, the heat radiating from the freezers kept it at a subtly high temperature.

The cool breeze reminded Max that despite how painful his memories were, they could change, much like the temperature. Similarly to the carnivorous foliage he had endured the situation and regained control.

"Do you want to go back to the car?"

Raymond asked in concern.

Max agreed.

When they got back to the car, Raymond checked in with Max about how he felt in the ice cream parlour. Popping the car door open and taking a seat, he began to eat his tub of ice cream and explained to Raymond that he had overheard the lads talking about the harbour.

"It sounded like they knew what was going on in there, I mean, is it common knowledge?"

He asked in concern.

Raymond slurped his milkshake before explaining,

"There have been rumours about squatters and criminal activity for months, they wrote about it in the paper and people have wanted answers. I'm going to be honest, once you checked in at the Hope Centre; I reported my concerns to the police. I left your name out of it; I knew you didn't want to talk about it, but, something needs to be done. With all the speculation, the police have had a lot of hoax calls and they don't seem to be bothering about it."

Max sighed deeply, continuing to eat his ice cream, aware he was once again trying to physically combat the psychological pain he was enduring. Making a conscious effort to fight his natural defence, he softly uttered the words

"I was raped."

As soon as he said it, his voice started to break. Raymond's face froze in stoic shock, looking to Max in both concern and horror.

Unable to repeat his statement, the car had transformed into a tense chamber of silence. The gears in the traumatised young man's head started to spin in a negative direction.

Still processing what he had heard, Raymond consoled Max and asked him if he wanted to talk about it, or go to the police.

"I've got nothing to go to the police with. I was unconscious when it happened and I have no idea who or how many people did it. No one's going to believe an addict, especially if I tell them that there was an old gangster down there running illegal fights, prostitution rings and numerous drug lines." Max exclaimed; pained and enraged by the predicament he was in.

Raymond calmly replied,

"I realise this is incredibly difficult situation and there is a lot of stuff to unpack and come to terms with. If, or when, you want to go to the police with this is up to you. But if you do want to report it I will support you."

Max sighed deeply and stared at his dull concrete surroundings out of the car window.

Sensing his young friend's feelings of hopelessness, Raymond asked,

"Fred told me that they kept you over night at the hospital. I'm assuming they gave you a looking over?"

Numbly nodding in agreement Max added,

"They had to stitch me up down there, I'm pretty sure they knew what happened."

Raymond continued to logically articulate how they could prove what had happened to him.

"They would have documented every injury; they wouldn't have been able to inform the police without you're say so. But if you report what's going on at the harbour, there will be evidence to back it up."

Max's focus drifted from his surroundings back toward Raymond, he started to realise that there was the potential of taking down another monster; a monster far more damaging than the heinous lie trap in his mind. Although he may never be able to know, or bring to justice, those who had violated him; he could identify the cruel and conniving kingpin that had facilitated it.

Max's memories about the harbour were clouded, but he knew that Candy-Shilling had orchestrated and profited from everything that was happening there. He found himself empowered with hope. Not only had he managed to start rebuilding himself, but he also had the ability to prevent similar experiences from happening to countless others.

By drawing the police to South Town Harbour he could help rebuild others lives and part of the city as a whole. Returning to his ice cream, Max felt mentally exhausted from the seemingly endless emotional rollercoaster he found himself on. His head became deadened to the anxieties and pain he had been carrying.

Raymond held the silence, recognising that he needed some time to process what had been going on.

After a few moments, the pregnant pause birthed a plan of action. He decided he wanted to report it to the police, armed with the knowledge that he would have the support of Raymond, The Hope Centre and St Catherine's Hospital. After reaching such an empowering and bold decision, his thoughts were drawn back to Fred.

He started to feel guilty that with all of the challenges the day had presented, the death of his mentor had faded to the back of his mind. However, after rising to so many challenges, he felt confident that he would be able to rise to the challenge of attending the funeral.

Once he had finished his ice cream he turned to Raymond and asked him to drive to the police station, where he could continue to reclaim the rest of his life and realign himself on the path to helping others once again.

AFTERMATH:

THE FOLLOWING NIGHT...

Back at the Harbour, Candy-Shilling was sat at his broken old desk. He was swigging a bottle of whisky into his rotten tooth decayed mouth, alone in the dark of night. The fight tank and the shag pile were operating as usual, but no one currently owed him anything so he had no interest in attending. Suddenly he heard a beeping noise.

"Bloody hell, who's that?"

He croaked, retrieving his old pager from his back pocket, silencing it before it attracted the attention from the pile of entranced or comatose zombies on the floor below.

As he peered into its screen he identified the number on it. Arising from his seat, he grabbed his cane and an old torch from his drawer, proceeding to hobble down the staircase. He shined the torch upward toward the ceiling, providing just enough light to see where he was going without awaking his brain dead customers.

Once clear of the building he found Sledge outside smoking.

"Oi love, open the hatch. We're going for a walk."

He barked at her. Without answering she obliged him and let him out of the condemned complex.

"Watch my back as I make this call" He scoffed as they got out. They made their way down the street to a vandalised old telephone box. Once they arrived, he cracked open the door the stench of urine emitted from the box. A tactic he had designed to ensure that it wouldn't be used by the general public. With the way Candy-Shilling led his life, he was immune to practically every foul smell imaginable. He picked up the receiver and dialled the number…

"Good evening officer. What can you do for me?"

He cackled.

"There's going to be a raid at the harbour on Friday, I can't stop it."

A nervous voice exclaimed.

"Well, thank you for being a friend. I'll make sure they don't find me… or your pictures there."

The voice frantically replied

"Please, I've helped you out here. I need to see those pictures destroyed."

"What are the filth looking for?"

Candy-Shilling sharply replied.

"Drugs, fight rings and prostitution rackets. Please… send me those photographs!"

"I'll be in touch about them in due time."

He snickered as he hung up the phone.

Candy-Shilling looked back at Sledge,

"Someone's grassed us; the old bill's coming down in two nights. You me and the Ring Master need to leave with the Tinks tonight!"

"What the hell do we need him for?" Sledge asked in disgust.

"He's the only other one that could grass us up. The

coppers will come down and find a pack of feral junkies and a load of drugs and we'll be in the clear. In a few months it'll all blow over and we can come back." Candy-Shilling sneered.

Dumbfounded at the idea of coming back Sledge asked

"Do you really think we can just come back after all that. They'll probably build something new there."

Candy-Shilling cackled

"I know things you don't know love, nothing's happening to that harbour while I'm around. Contacts and leverage are all you need in life."

END

Want more?

Explore more of the Sea-Side City Timeline in:

Sea-Side City

The Tides of Change Compilation

Includes 6 stories in 1 book!

Available on Amazon Books

For more information visit:
www.saballantyne.com

SEA-SIDE CITY
TIMELINE

2011

UNTOLD LEGEND

Starts: October 2011

Ends: April 2012

NIGHT COAT: ORIGINS

Starts: October 2011

Ends: May 2012

2012

LIFE IN THE RUINS

Starts: April 2012

Ends: June 2012

POLITICAL LIABILITIES

Starts: May 2012

Ends: May 2012

SURVEYING THE TERRITORY

Starts: June 2012

Ends: June 2012

CIRCLE OF LIFE

Starts: June 2012

Ends: June 2012

THE FRAGILE MASK OF PORCELAIN

Starts: July 2012

Ends: July 2012

????

S.A. BALLANTYNE'S VISION:

Night-Desk Publications (NDP) aims to produce a range of unique, fictional story content, offering social commentaries and a range of different genres.

Additionally, it will offer innovative means through which readers can engage with its content.

The philosophy behind these aims is that people can often benefit from engaging with information in different ways. NDP values individuality and innovation, therefore, Night Desk Publications products will offer interactive websites to enhance the reader's experience.

(Starting with the Sea-Side City universe)

Kind Regards

S.A. Ballantyne

Keep in touch...

@BallantyneNdp

www.saballantyne.com

CARNINGSDALE

KINGS-PORT HARBOUR

CITY OF ROCKSHORE

OUTSKIRTS

Stockbridge Finances

St. Catherine's Hospital

The Messenger Printing Office

Lou's News

Rockshore Train Station

NORTH SIDE

St. Catherine's Church

Community Centre

CITY CENTRE

Coastal-Collage Shopping Centre

The Job Centre

University Library

Penelope Park

Town Square

Cabot's Court Flats

"Cone-ee-Island" Ice Cream Parlour

Town Hall

Town Cryer Pub (The TC)

"Jacksville" Winstone-Way Council Estate

Audrey's Tea-Rooms

Parson's Care Home

"The Port in a Storm" Pub

Old Club House

Raven's-Dale Road (Pubs and Clubs)

Shopping Precinct (Cutting Craft Location)

INDUSTRIAL AREA

South Town Harbour (Condemned)

Student Halls of Residence

SOUTH SIDE

Family Funfair

High End Sea-View Housing

Seafront

Ferryport

Welcome to the Sea-Side City

COCKLESHORE ISLE (Neighbouring Island)

Return to the

Sea-Side City

LOST AT SEA

The second entry in:

The Sands of Time Compilation

DCI Kent revisits his past in hopes of gaining more insight into identifying the Sex-Doll Killer

Coming soon

www.saballantyne.com

Printed in Great Britain
by Amazon